High Crag Linn

Human life is very cheap in fifteenth-century England. Hawk Jankin and his band of outlaws are looting, killing and laying waste to the countryside. Anna's father is away fighting in the war, and she and her mother are left to protect their castle.

Hawk will not give up his demands for the castle, once owned by his family, and for Anna to marry him. So she agrees, despite everyone's warnings. She thinks it will make things better – but what happens next is even more terrible. High Crag Linn, which has been the silent witness of many violent deaths, awaits more. Hawk wants revenge for his thwarted ambition. He can order murder, but he cannot escape the haunting nightmare of what he has done and the regret for his loss.

How can you forgive people when they have done their worst to you? How is it possible to stop hating when your life and the lives of all those around you have been ruined?

Most difficult of all: how do you forgive yourself?

Margaret McAllister is the author of several children's novels. She lives in Yorkshire with her husband and has three grown-up children. Her interests include dance, theatre, music and escaping into the countryside.

For Tony, Adam, Elinor and Iain,
who came with me to so many waterfalls.

A special thank you to Elinor, who taught me
that going uphill is easier if you walk backwards.

HIGH CRAG LINN

MARGARET McALLISTER

LION
CHILDREN'S

Text copyright © 2007 Margaret McAllister

The moral rights of the author
have been asserted

A Lion Children's Book
an imprint of
Lion Hudson plc
Wilkinson House, Jordan Hill Road,
Oxford OX2 8DR, England
www.lionhudson.com
ISBN: 978-0-7459-6062-3

First edition 2007
1 3 5 7 9 10 8 6 4 2 0

A catalogue record for this book is available
from the British Library

Typeset in 11/14 Elegant Garamond BT
Printed and bound in Great Britain
by Cox and Wyman Ltd, Reading

The text paper used in this book has been made from wood
independently certified as having come from sustainable forests.

Hawk Jankin at High Crag Tower,
Two maidens at Hollylaw;
The price of peace was a flower
That flowered nevermore.

And what became of the shadow?
And what became of the bride?
And what became of Jankin,
Who led the fiery ride?

Oh, one was lost in water,
And one in fire and pain,
And one went up to High Crag Linn
And never came back again.

Prologue

It was not always like this. If you go to Hollylaw in summer today, you find a gleam of cars jostling to park in the market place because the visitors love it so much. They would like to live in this village with its ruined castle on the top of the hill, its weathered old church at the bottom and stone cottages in between. Bright flowers trail from hanging baskets and windowboxes. There are antique and bric-a-brac shops, a delicatessen, a bookshop called Holly Leaves, the Lillie Arms Hotel with a bar called Jankin's Lair, and the Flower of Hollylaw Gift Shop and Tea Rooms, where a girl and her mother are finishing their iced drinks. The mother browses among the postcards and pretty paper napkins while the girl goes to explore the village. She is fourteen, on holiday, and has not been here before.

She wanders down to the church, imagining this village in the past, not noticing that that she is walking over a flagstone with something carved into one corner. It is old and worn, and could be a flower. A lily? In the coolness of the church with its smell of flowers and furniture polish, she picks up a leaflet, photocopied on yellow paper, which gives the story of the village.

The most well-known and poignant story of Hollylaw is of Anna, 'the Flower of Hollylaw'. She was the only daughter of the Lord of the Manor, Sir Hugh Lillie, and his wife, Lady Isabel. Hollylaw, being in a wild and remote part of the north, was threatened by a gang of outlaws led by Hawk Jankin, whose family had been the overlords in the past. In the Wars of the Roses, Sir Hugh, his only son (also named Hugh) and most of the able-bodied men had gone to fight on King Richard's side, so the village was poorly defended. Hawk Jankin and his men attacked ruthlessly. Anybody who defied them was taken to High Crag Linn waterfall and hurled down onto the rocks to die. Anna Lillie was believed at this time to be about fourteen years old, which, at that time, was considered old enough to marry.

Fourteen, thinks the girl. *Like me.*

Chapter One

High Crag Tower. Hawk Jankin looked down from a dim, grim room that smelled of sweat and leather. His hair was red and wild, coarse ginger hairs grew thickly on his arms and the backs of his hands, and his leather jerkin and boots were hard worn. From a slit of a window in the rough stone he could see six men tramping up the steep hill, three of them leading horses. The tower was cool, but outside the sun was strong and the laden horses glistened with sweat. The trapdoor in the floor banged open and shut again, but Jankin did no more than glance over his shoulder as his kinsman Falcon strode to his side.

Falcon's boots creaked and the sword at his side swayed. Long dark hair straggled down his back. He was a little taller than Jankin, and stretched to look over the top of his head.

'Are they bringing the Hollylaw harvest?' he asked idly. 'We may as well have it. We already have their sheep.'

'*Our* sheep,' said Jankin. 'Our sheep, our cattle and our harvest. It's all ours by right, and we'll have it again.'

'Soon?' asked Falcon. He was almost smiling, which was a rare thing for Falcon.

'Very soon,' said Jankin. 'With the fighting men away, they can't hold against us. We took horses last week, we went back for the sheep, we're carrying off their harvest, and they haven't even followed.'

'That's because they know about High Crag Linn and don't want to end up at the bottom of it,' observed Falcon calmly. 'It's my guess that Lady Isabel won't send for help any more. The bottom of the Linn could get dammed up with bodies. Mind, I didn't push the last one down the Linn. He was more trouble than he was worth so I left him dead on the moors, but it's gey hot for leaving a body lying around. If you think Hollylaw is ours for the taking, why don't we take it now?'

Jankin grinned as he examined his grimy fingernails. 'We could take Hollylaw tonight,' he said. 'We could take it any time, but it's not enough to take it by force. We need to hold it by lawful right so nobody can ever take it from us.'

There was still a smile on his face as he turned to face Falcon – the smile of the man who throws a pair of loaded dice and knows he has already won.

'I have Hollylaw and the castle in my hand,' he said. 'The chances are that Sir Hugh and his son will not come back alive from this war. We can make sure they don't, if we have to. With neither of them left, it will pass to –'

'Young Anna! But she's only a lassie!' exclaimed Falcon.

'She's old enough to wed,' replied Jankin. 'And she's a beauty.'

'The mother won't have it,' said Falcon.

'It's not the mother I want,' said Jankin, and their laughter scared the crows from the battlements above them. 'We'll do this properly. I'm the true Lord of Hollylaw, and that's what they're going to see. When we ride to Hollylaw, you and I must look like knights from the court. Anna might be scared of marrying me, but she won't be ashamed. Falcon, be my ambassador. Take a gift – there's a silver chain we got from somewhere – take that, take an escort, give my regards to Lady Isabel and tell her I want to marry her daughter. Give her a day, then go back for her answer.'

Falcon jumped back down through the trapdoor, scattering the rats below. Striding towards the spring to wash, unlacing his jerkin, he heard the clink and creak of harness. The sweaty horses and sweatier men were bringing Hollylaw's harvest to Jankin's store.

Chapter Two

'He couldn't even come himself!' snarled Lady Isabel. 'He sent Falcon!'

In the Great Hall of the castle, Lady Isabel Lillie and Anna faced each other from either end of the long wooden table, pressing their hands down on it, leaning towards each other, their eyes as sharp as sparrowhawks'. Thomasin the maid stood respectfully at a distance, her hands neatly folded in front of her old russet gown, her wild black curls scraped back and fastened under her cap. She couldn't help thinking that she had seen cats squaring up to each other like this, snarling for a fight.

The hall was cool, for the dense stone walls held out the sunshine. The ceiling was high and vast, the windows small and the light dim. Wooden chests and benches stood against the walls, and a faded tapestry hung on one wall. The only brightness in the room was Anna. Her gown used to be deep red and had faded to pink but it stood out like a flower in ashes, and her hair hung down her back in pale gold. It was Thomasin's responsibility to make sure that Anna looked her best, and the maid was pleased with her work.

Outside, the blacksmith's wee daughter was still wailing in a voice far too loud for such a little dot. Jankin's raiders had carried off their chickens, and the lassie's own pet hen was missing. The blacksmith's sons who were too young to go to war were out on watch, ready to give warning of Jankin's men

11

riding down from the hills; *may God help them*, thought Thomasin, *they're only boys*. Each evening, when Thomasin brushed Anna's golden hair, there was less and less to talk about, apart from Jankin, and who'd want to talk about him? The thought of him made Thomasin feel bitter at heart. If she could deliver them all from his threat by pushing him down the Linn and his lackey Falcon after him she would, but as it was she could only watch Anna and Lady Isabel glaring at each other across the table. This could take a while. She knew them well enough to know that neither would give in.

'Of course I don't want to marry Jankin!' insisted Anna. 'In a time of peace he wouldn't dare to ask! But this is a time of war, and in times of war things are not normal.'

'That's why we must fight to keep them as normal as possible,' replied her mother. 'It will not always be like this.'

Holy Saint Anne, thought Thomasin, *you can tell those two are mother and daughter.*

'What else can save us until Father and the men return?' demanded Anna. 'And when will that be, and what if they don't return at all? Meanwhile, there are raids by day and night, and the animals we have left are all crammed into our own courtyard because they're not safe anywhere else. What do we feed them on when Jankin's men steal the hay? If I marry him, it will stop.'

'So he says,' snapped Lady Isabel. 'If you believe him, you've been in the sun too long.'

'He *will* stop,' said Anna, very firmly and calmly. 'That's the whole point of marrying me. He'll have what he wants, so he'll stop, and when Father and Hugh come home, they'll settle him.'

'They could send him limping back to High Crag Tower,' snapped her mother, 'but you'd still be his wife.'

Ah, but Sir Hugh could make her a widow, thought Thomasin, but it wasn't her place to speak.

'And if your father and Hugh don't come home?' went on Lady Isabel. 'You've a cousin in Kent who might have a better claim to the manor than a daughter. If your father doesn't come home, your cousin might inherit Hollylaw and turn you out, but you'd still be married to Jankin.'

Aye, but your cousin could make you a widow, thought Thomasin.

'If King Richard wins the war, he'll help us,' said Anna, stubbornly keeping her temper.

The king's hangman could make you a widow, thought Thomasin.

'And if Henry Tudor wins the war?' demanded her mother. 'He could give the manor to anyone. We'd have nothing, and you'd *still* be married to Jankin!'

Then I'd just have to make you a widow myself, thought Thomasin, remembering all that Hollylaw had endured from Jankin. Hungry days, stolen beasts, stolen crops, murdered friends. Dead or dying, they lay in the waters at the bottom of High Crag Linn.

Living in the caves behind the waterfall was a hermit, a holy man who cared for the dying. One man in Hollylaw had been rescued from the rocks by the hermit, nursed back to health and sent home, but he had been the only one to survive. He never spoke of what had happened.

Nobody in Hollylaw slept well any more, and it wasn't the hot summer nights that kept them awake. It was fear.

'If you wed him, you wed him for life,' said Lady Isabel.

'And what sort of life will we all have if I don't wed him?' asked Anna calmly. 'What sort of life will all the people of this village have?'

Lady Isabel banged down her two hands on the table. 'They'll have the best I can give them!' she cried. 'Haven't your father and I taken care of them? That evil hill wolf isn't having Hollylaw, and he isn't having you.'

'But Mother,' cried Anna, 'we can't protect ourselves from him!'

'How dare you argue!' thundered Lady Isabel. 'I sent that Falcon away and I should have twisted his stolen silver round his neck. Thomasin! Keep my daughter out of my sight or I swear I'll take a whip to her!'

She banged the table once more, took her gown in one hand and marched away with her head high. The men outside were already waiting to put down the bedding in the Great Hall, so Thomasin followed Anna down the stairs and into the courtyard with its hot, strong smell of animals.

Thomasin had been with Anna since they were little girls. Her father and mother had both been good servants of the family; when she had been left an orphan, Lady Isabel and Sir Hugh had taken her under their protection to be Anna's maid. She and Anna had shared every happiness and misery. As children they had explored each inch of the castle, climbed in and out of every window, up and down every ladder, and through every trapdoor from ramparts to cellar. They had even tried in vain to climb chimneys. If Anna was ill, Thomasin looked after her. If Thomasin was ill, Anna was ordered not to go near her, but she would wait until a servant opened the door, then slip in and refuse to move, risking infection and a whipping for disobedience.

They shared Anna's clothes, her dogs, her horse. Thomasin had nothing to share but her love, her wit, her hard work and her fighting spirit, and she shared those generously. She sometimes thought they shared Anna's goodness, too, for she wasn't sure she had any of her own, but determination was something they both possessed in every vein. The servants said it was a good thing those two never fell out, for there was no giving way in either of them.

'We never quarrel,' said Thomasin. 'If we don't agree, we throw dice.' Anna carried the dice in the velvet bag at her waist, but they didn't often need them.

'We can't continue like this,' said Anna. She gathered her gown to keep it from trailing on the stairs. 'Jankin won't harm the manor if he thinks it will be his one day.'

'And how will he treat us all if you marry him and make him our overlord?' demanded Thomasin, flapping the flies away as they stepped into the sunny courtyard, steering Anna away from the cow muck. 'If you make him Lord of the Manor, he can do what he likes.'

'He'll do what he likes anyway,' said Anna.

'We'll go down fighting,' said Thomasin. 'We won't let him have you. Come away from the cows, Anna. You may plan to live among brute beasts, but you needn't start now.'

While Anna and Thomasin slept that night, Mistress Isabel didn't go to her bed. She prepared to defend her home. Wrapped in her cloak under a night sky spread with stars, she paced the battlements and sent for Will, the blacksmith. He had served the family all his life, and had the strength of ten men in each huge shoulder. More importantly, she called for Alan, the steward. Like Will, he was too slow and stiff now for the war, but he was a giant of a man with the muscles of an ox, the fist of a smith and a round shining head that he had to bow to walk through the doorways. They both offered to leave the manor to send for help, but Lady Isabel would have none of that. They must not be caught and flung down High Crag Linn.

The next morning brought a wisp of a breeze. Lady Isabel
stood tall on the drawbridge, stern as a standing stone on the
moors, watching as riders worked their way down the hill.
Alan and Will flanked her. Anna and Thomasin were not
allowed to be there, so they squashed together at the tiny
window of a guard tower, looking down as Falcon and his
escort rode down the hill to receive Lady Isabel's answer.
Hooves pounded on dry ground and dust flew as Falcon rode
through the village. Children and animals fled.

With his escort behind him, Falcon cantered through the
village and up to the drawbridge, holding the reins in one
hand for show, dark hair flying behind him until he clattered
to a halt to face Lady Isabel. She stood firm, not turning away
though the dust blew into her eyes. In the tower, Anna and
Thomasin pressed together, taking turns to get a good view.

'Who does he think he is?' muttered Thomasin.

'Good morrow, Lady Isabel!' called Falcon, but she didn't
reply. 'Hawk Jankin will have what is rightfully his. He'll have
it in peace, with Anna as an honourable bride, or he'll have it
knee deep in blood, but he'll have it, lady.'

Lady Isabel tilted up her chin. 'Tell your Jankin to come
here himself,' she called, 'instead of sending his wild-haired
weasel. Tell him to get off his stolen horse and fight man to
man for Hollylaw. Alan will be my champion, but I see Jankin
would rather fight with women and children.'

Alan strode forward and folded his arms.

'Alan the Steward?' said Falcon, with a laugh that was
almost a bark. 'Is the old dancing bear all you can offer?
Jankin may as well fight Lady Anna's maid. He makes the
rules, not you, lady. He is of noble blood, and won't stoop to

brawling with a servant. Madam, he dearly longs to marry your daughter. He will give her all the honour and wealth she should have as the Lady of Hollylaw, but I'll tell him he'll have to work harder to win her.' He turned his horse's head and wheeled away.

'There will be a battle,' whispered Anna. 'It will be terrible.'

Thomasin, wrapping her arms round Anna, wanted to spit Falcon's words back into his face. *Fight Lady Anna's maid. You're welcome. You'd see what the maid can do.*

At High Crag Tower, weapons clanked and rang. The forge fire blazed. The smell of heat, sweat and metal and the ruthless clang of the hammer made it a vision of hell. The men tasted the chance of a fight like blood in their mouths and power in their veins. The horses stamped and tossed their heads, spreading fear amongst them.

At Hollylaw, the beasts, the folk and all the harvest they could store were crammed into the castle. Archers were set on the ramparts, day and night. Oil and water were ready for heating and pouring down the walls. Serving women learned to shoot. Nerves were tight as bowstrings, sharp as arrow points.

Alan the Steward and Lady Isabel watched from the guard room over the gate. Anna and Thomasin were not to go near the battlements, so they huddled by the small window of the bedchamber and watched as the sky darkened, and nothing happened.

And nothing happened.

And nothing happened.

'Don't bite your nails, Thomasin,' said Anna.

Thomasin took her fingertip from her mouth. 'Don't twist your hair,' she said.

'Anyone would think we were afraid,' said Anna, and they giggled awkwardly. They knew it was no time for laughter, but somehow they couldn't help it. A spindle, with a little cloud of fleece and a long thread, hung from Thomasin's waist, and she twirled it steadily. Anna took out the dice and they played until Anna grew tired. Thomasin brushed Anna's hair, helped her into her nightgown and pulled the bed curtains round her, then wrapped herself in a cloak at the window and lit candles. Still nothing happened. She peeped round the bed curtains to see if Anna had fallen asleep, but Anna was on her knees with her rosary beads in her hands and a look about her as if she might be hundreds of miles away in a place where Thomasin couldn't reach her. Then they heard the first scream.

The night was so dark that hills and sky were of equal blackness with flames leaping against it, torch after torch after torch after torch, moving down to Hollylaw. Harsh wild shouts were cried out like the yelping of wild beasts, closer and closer to the fields.

The line of fire stopped. Flames and smoke blew across the sky, but they came no nearer.

'Lady Isabel!' Jankin's voice carried, loud and strong. 'We seek an honourable marriage. All I have taken from Hollylaw will be restored, and Anna will bring peace to the manor. But it is my manor, and to stand in my way is to stand in the way of justice.'

The wind whipped at Lady Isabel's words, but Thomasin and Anna heard them. 'Is it justice to hurl my people down the waterfall, hell hawk?'

The first flight of arrows sang from the battlements. The torches dipped. A line of flame flickered along the ground, then another and another as if someone were drawing lines along the earth. There was one more to the right and one to the left. It crackled, then roared. Jankin and his men were burning fields, barns and livestock. Greedy flames gobbled their way to fences and homes. Cruel smoke filled the air with choking.

'Help me with my gown,' ordered Anna. Thomasin laced her into her dress and reached for the hairbrush, but Anna was already on her way down to the Great Hall, where the people of Hollylaw had gathered. Thomasin followed with a candle.

'I have to do something,' said Anna. 'I have to comfort them.' But in the Great Hall, there were no tears.

Many people were still asleep on the floor, curled together or sprawled alone in the smell of hot heavy bodies and clothes worn all summer. Those awake were clustered together, drinking weak ale, telling jokes and laughing, though when they saw the Flower of Hollylaw step into the hall with her long gown gathered in her hand, they suddenly stopped. Some were pressed up against the slits in the stone, listening. Now and again there came a cry and a roar of fire and they scowled and even winced, but nobody wept. They heard another singing of arrows from the battlements, then a cry of pain.

'Was that Jankin we got?' asked someone.

'Doubt we'd have such luck,' said a man with a front tooth missing. He turned a crooked grin towards Anna. 'Don't you worry, Flower. He'll not get near you. You go to your bed.'

'I'll stay,' said Anna, and drew back with Thomasin to a dark corner where sleepers snored and grunted. 'It's all wrong,' she said. 'I should be protecting them, not the other way round. I should care for them.' But there was little to do in a long night. A child woke crying from a nightmare and Anna rocked it in her lap until it fell asleep in her arms.

When the sun was up, they traipsed up the stairs. The

smell of burning reached them like grim news. From the battlements it seemed as if the clouds had dropped from heaven and landed on little Hollylaw, for grey was everywhere, the grey of ash and the grey of smouldering. The lowing of stolen beasts reached them from far up the hill. Alan the Steward arrived with sweat and dirt on his face and rage in his eyes.

'They've driven off every beast that was left outside,' he said. 'What's more, they've put a torch to the thatch of my mother's cottage. She's sheltering here, so I've yet to tell her.'

'I don't understand,' said Thomasin. 'If Jankin wants the village for his own, why is he destroying it?'

'Why should he care?' demanded Alan sourly. 'It's the land he wants. He'll be content so long as he has a place for his men to drink, somewhere for the animals he's stolen and good stabling for the horses so he can ride out and steal some more. If he sat himself down here as Lord of the Manor, it wouldn't be his own men who'd go short of anything. He's laying waste to the village, but he wouldn't care for it, not even if he were sitting here in Sir Hugh's chair.'

The next night, Anna stayed in her clothes and watched. Flames roared and rushed from the church. In the castle they heard its glass shatter. It felt like the breaking of their own bones, they were so proud of that glass. Anna shuddered, and Thomasin hugged her.

'It'll go on like this,' said Anna. 'He'll go on until there's nothing left.' She shook herself like a waking cat. 'Thomasin, bring my white mantle. We'll need torches.'

Thomasin wrapped the mantle round her, but Anna's voice had sounded remote and colourless in the dark, as if she were walking and talking in her sleep. She took a torch from the wall bracket and held it to look into Anna's face.

Yes, she thought. *She is far away from me. But she isn't sleepwalking.*

Anna's face was as set as if she had been carved in marble to last for ever. Sorrow hung round her. Coldness shivered down Thomasin's arms as she understood what Anna meant to do.

'Don't, my lady,' she said. 'Please, my lady, Anna, please, don't.'

Anna turned at last, and managed to smile. 'It's the only way,' she said. 'Do you think I can endure any more of what he's doing to our people? Can they bear any more? I can offer a chance of peace, so how can I not do it?'

'But to marry him, Anna! Stop and think about it!' Then Thomasin wished she hadn't said that, because of course Anna had thought about it. She had done nothing but think about it, day and night.

'Will you come with me?' asked Anna.

'If you must,' said Thomasin. 'Of course I'll come with you. Anywhere.'

Anna squared her shoulders and lifted her chin. 'We should take two torches,' she said.

We'll either make a great impression on them or both be shot through the heart, thought Thomasin. Each holding a torch high in one hand, they lifted their skirts and climbed the spiral staircase until they stood at the strong wooden door that led to the battlements.

'Excuse me, madam, I'll do this,' said Thomasin. She heaved the door open and, taking great care with the burning torch, held her hair with her free hand to keep the bushy curls from catching fire. She stepped out to a breath of wind that caught the flame, streaming it back from her – but the same wind was drawing Jankin's fires towards them, hungry orange tongues leaning to taste the castle. Letting go of her hair, she leaned against the door to hold it for Anna.

Jankin's voice, harsh with smoke, cried out from the fire.

'We will do no more tonight, Lady Isabel. But we will have your answer.'

Thomasin and Anna stood under a sky of deep velvet. Smoke crept across it. Beyond the village, fields muttered with burning. Thomasin, who had often run across this roof with Anna, wondered why it seemed such a vast, frightening place now. Perhaps it was because Anna was about to take the longest journey of her life. Anna held her torch high above her white mantle.

'You can still go back,' said Thomasin.

'I can't,' said Anna. 'Step up with me to the battlements.'

'Get away, my lady!' roared an archer. 'You'll be shot, madam!'

'And you'll be hanged,' retorted Thomasin. An arrow box lay against the ramparts, and she tested it with her foot. 'That'll take your weight. Anna. Watch what you're doing with that torch.'

Anna climbed on to the arrow box and raised the torch as high as her arm could reach. Stretching on tiptoe because the arrow box might not bear both of them, Thomasin did the same.

'They haven't seen us,' said Thomasin. *Perhaps they won't. With any luck this will prove to be a ridiculous idea and we'll go back down the stairs as if nothing had happened. Even now, I might talk Anna out of it.* But Falcon's voice rang from the fire, and Thomasin hated him for it.

'Hawk! Tower!'

Hawk Jankin held out his arm to silence his men. A slender white figure stood on the tower in a flare of torchlight. She was shouting something – two voices were shouting – cursing the crackle of burning and the tearful wailing, Jankin rode to the moat with Falcon at his side.

'It's the lasses!' said Falcon. 'Calling to speak!'

'She wants me,' grinned Jankin. 'What did I tell you? She can't wait.'

He had ridden as close as he could to the water's edge, with armed men around him. On both sides, bows were drawn.

'We'll speak!' shouted Jankin. Voices died away. In the courtyard, defenders gazed up at the battlements. Some thought a fiery angel had come to defend them, and crossed themselves. When they saw that it was only Anna, they still stared.

On the roof, Anna glanced over her shoulder.

'My mother will be up soon,' she said.

'I bolted the door,' said Thomasin. 'But you'd better be quick.'

Anna took a deep breath. She would have to shout with all her lungs.

'Hawk Jankin!' she cried. Jankin raised a mailed fist to show that he heard her.

'Jankin,' shouted Anna, and though the winds tossed the words about, everyone heard her. 'Spare Hollylaw!' She slowed down, to give every word strength. 'Spare Hollylaw, and for peace I WILL MARRY YOU!'

Jankin leapt from his horse. 'No man of mine will harm Hollylaw again!' he shouted back. 'Your beasts will be returned! Your houses will be rebuilt! For the great honour done me by the Flower of Hollylaw, there will be peace!'

On the roof, someone was banging and hammering at the door. Lady Isabel was calling for an axe.

'I will return in the morning,' yelled Jankin, 'to speak to Lady Isabel.'

'And on my word of honour, you will leave unharmed,' called Anna. Wood splintered behind her, and she leaned forward to shout. 'I say again, for the peace of Hollylaw, I will marry you!'

Chapter Three

Anna jumped in alarm as the door crashed behind her, but Thomasin shielded her. Will the Smith forced his way through the torn wood, pushed Thomasin out of the way as if she were a skittle, and seized Anna round the waist, throwing the torch over the battlements. Thomasin sprang forward to defend her, but Alan the Steward had clambered in through the hacked door, wrenched the torch from her hand, and held her back as Will dragged Anna away. Bundled down the stairs after her, Thomasin could hear kicks and cries as Anna struggled. She could hear, too, the sharp voice of Lady Isabel.

'Don't hurt her, Will!' ordered Lady Isabel. 'Lock her in, but don't hurt her! Thomasin!'

At the bottom of the stairs, Alan dragged Thomasin into the darkness. There was just time to hear three footsteps and the swish of a skirt before torchlight shone in her eyes, and a smash across her face threw her so wildly off balance that if Alan had not been holding her she would have fallen sprawling on the floor.

'Pardon me, madam, but it's not Thomasin's fault,' said Alan, but Lady Isabel grabbed her by the shoulders.

'How dare you betray me, Thomasin? Did you tell her to do it? Or did you just hold the torch for her? She'll not marry him, but I've been made to look a fool in front of Jankin's men and my own. Why didn't you stop her?'

Thomasin struggled to speak. Lady Isabel had hit the breath out of her.

'Please, my lady,' she panted, 'there was no stopping her.'

The rings on Lady Isabel's hand flashed in the torchlight as she slapped Thomasin again. Alan held Thomasin more gently.

'You should have come to me!' snarled Lady Isabel. 'I would have stopped her! I shouted after them that they were not having Anna whatever she said, but they rode off pretending not to hear. We will have to start all over again. You'd think she'd been bewitched.'

'No, madam, please, madam,' gasped Thomasin, 'please, there are ways of managing this. *Please*, madam.' She tried to look into Lady Isabel's eyes, though her own were watering so badly that they blurred. 'May I speak?'

Lady Isabel stared coldly at her. 'Come with me,' she ordered. 'Alan, don't let us be disturbed.'

Alan released Thomasin and patted her shoulder. Thomasin dried her eyes on her sleeve and followed Lady Isabel. For a moment she thought they were going into the chapel, but soon she realized that they were on their way to the small solar chamber beside it. Lady Isabel pushed aside the hanging over the door so roughly that its rings clattered, put the torch in a bracket on the walls, lit a candle from it and said sternly, 'Speak, Thomasin.'

'My lady,' said Thomasin, 'if Anna *will* marry him, I can do the thing we want most.'

She lowered her voice. The fear of what she was about to say overawed her.

'Do you hate him as much as I do?' she asked softly. She saw in Lady Isabel's eyes that it was unnecessary even to ask.

'Madam,' Thomasin whispered, 'we all want him dead. We can't kill him from a distance.'

Lady Isabel lowered her eyes and looked steadily at the candle as if she expected it to speak to her. Then she looked at Thomasin again.

'Go on, girl,' she said.

'If she marries him and goes to High Crag Tower,' said Thomasin, 'I'll have to go with her. She'll still need me. I'll have the best chance any of us could have. Let her marry him, madam, and give me a sharp knife or poison. I promise you, I will make her a widow or die trying. You could ask her to do it herself, madam, but she wouldn't. She's too good, but I'm not.'

Lady Isabel's face showed nothing. No surprise, no pleasure, no shock.

'It will be harder than you think,' she said. 'And if you fail, I doubt you'll get a second chance.'

'I know,' said Thomasin. Lady Isabel still did not smile, but Thomasin felt the approval in the strong gaze.

'Stay there,' said Lady Isabel quietly. She glided to the door, spoke quietly to Alan and left the room while Thomasin warmed her fingertips at the candle flame and delicately touched her face. There was no tenderness, so perhaps she wouldn't be bruised and Anna would not have to know that Lady Isabel had hit her so hard.

Lady Isabel returned with a covered basket in her arms. Her face was as set as granite.

'Pay attention, Thomasin,' she said, very softly.

It was three more hours before dawn spread across the sky and lit the bitter cloud of smoke. Anna, drawn and exhausted, had prayed until prayer felt hopeless as ashes. Now she lay empty and listless across the bed, wondering when somebody would come for her and hoping it would be Thomasin. When she had called out for help somebody had brought her milk, but nobody had told her anything, and she had been locked in again while servants and serfs shared gossip of what had happened the night before.

'She did, I saw her. She stood on the roof.'

'She must have been bewitched.'

'Aye, she was.'

'Aye, there was a dark imp behind her.'

'That was Thomasin, you fool.'

'Mistress Anna wouldn't have promised that. It's my guess she went up there to shout curses at him. They all heard her wrong.'

'Curses? From our Flower?'

'That wasn't her. That was an angel.'

'Was it? Then an angel just said it would marry Hawk Jankin.'

'Shut your filthy godless mouth! The poor little Flower's been locked up all night. Have you seen Lady Isabel? She's spitting hell fire. I hear she beat the lights out of Thomasin. Here's Alan, he'll know. Alan, what's happening?'

Alan ducked under the low doorway. His face was serious, and they had a feeling that he knew more than he was saying.

'How's Lady Isabel?'

'How's Anna?'

'What about Thomasin? What's happening?'

'What about the work you have to do?' said Alan, and he marched resolutely away. There would be a wedding feast to prepare, if there were any beasts worth slaughtering.

Was it morning already? Thomasin had been up all night. There had been so much to learn, and Lady Isabel seemed satisfied with the way she had understood her lessons.

She felt much older than Anna now. She understood about keys and bolts, knives and daggers, poison and how to administer it. She had considered all the ways to conceal the tiny silver vials and small, keen daggers Lady Isabel had given her. She would need two bottles of poison because Falcon must die too. The men might rally round him if he were left alive.

Whatever girlhood she had taken with her into the solar chamber, she decided to leave it behind. Proudly she followed Lady Isabel from the room, and nobody dared to speak to them as they swept towards the bedchamber where Anna sat hugging her knees.

'You will marry him,' said Lady Isabel, wrapping Anna in her arms and looking over her daughter's head at Thomasin. 'It will be for the best, and Thomasin will always look after you.'

'It will be for the best,' said Anna earnestly. 'Jankin doesn't know any other life than the way he lives now. There must be some good in him, and I have to bring it out.'

Thomasin managed a twitch of a smile. The less said the better.

If the people of Hollylaw did not believe what they heard – that Lady Isabel had agreed to the marriage – they believed what they saw when Jankin's men drove their lowing, bleating, stolen beasts back to the battered village. Alan selected the ones to be killed and discreetly sent a message to Thomasin that she was to help the head slaughterman. The slaughterman may have wondered why Thomasin had to practise the art of driving a knife into a heart and whipping it out as quickly and cleanly as possible, but he asked no questions. He taught her, watched her and was eventually satisfied that she could do it well enough.

In the next two days Lady Isabel tried by force of will and imploring prayer to drag her husband and son home from the war. Anna prayed for a miracle. The castle and the village were flung into a frenzy of work, rebuilding homes as far as they could, scouring the smoke-scarred land for whatever they could find. Jankin had returned their beasts fat and healthy. The grazing lands had been badly trampled and scorched, but Jankin had returned the stolen hay too.

Some said it was too good to be true, and some said it was good enough to be going on with. Whatever happened next, there would be a few good days to restore, to mend, to stop being afraid. In the castle, there was food to prepare, there were gowns to be brushed and mended, horses to be groomed, chambers to be swept and strewn. They must put on a good show for this wedding, if only for themselves, for Lady Isabel swore that Hawk Jankin and his thieves would not set foot in her house. The celebration would take place in the open air, in the churchyard.

Thomasin had more to do than anyone, which, they said, must be why she had that look about her as if she were always thinking of something else. Sir Hugh had given Anna a gown of pale sky blue at the New Year before last and Thomasin had taken great care of it, storing it in woodruff and tansy to keep away the moths. Not only was it beautiful, but everyone knew how rare and expensive it was. Thomasin lifted it gently from the chest, shook out the herbs, and held it to the light.

It would need altering again, as Anna's shape had changed considerably in the last eighteen months. Thomasin sat in the light by the window, unpicking seams, turning and measuring, pinning and sewing, all the time rehearsing in her head what she must do to hold a dagger effectively and to administer a poison so it would not be tasted. She wished she knew her way out of High Crag Tower. All day she sewed, altering Anna's gown and her own, brushing and mending Lady Isabel's, and finally stitching jewels onto Anna's bodice. This gave her an idea which she suggested to Lady Isabel, who gave her silver coins to stitch into their hems in case they needed to bribe their way out of trouble. As the sun shone higher and then lower, she moved from window to window, angling her work against the shadows, resenting the unstoppable rolling of the hours that would bring Anna's wedding day.

'Try this on,' she said at last, and Anna, pale and listless, slipped her arms into the gown and stood still as Thomasin laced and tugged and smoothed. 'You should eat something.'

'The reek from the kitchens is foul,' said Anna.

'All the better,' muttered Thomasin, and tugged viciously at a shoulder seam. 'You might eat something bad and be too ill to marry him.'

'I can't,' said Anna. 'Don't argue. I can't eat anything today.' Her voice faltered to a whisper. 'I almost wish I weren't doing this. I keep reminding myself that Jankin can change, but he needs help to change. I'm doing it for peace.'

'And peace is what we'll have,' said Thomasin, ramming a pin into place.

Chapter Four

The sun shone on the morning of Anna's wedding. It poured through the windows of the solar chamber, where she stood in her gown of heaven blue, her fair hair brushed long and loose and crowned with a cap of pearls. Thomasin, having dressed her, stood back and was pleased with her work. Anna looked like an angel, and Thomasin's angel was not to be thrown to a demon with hair the colour of hell fire. Again and again they glanced to check the height of the sun, listening for a call or the sound of hooves, finding little to say and wishing it were over, exchanging twitches of smiles to reassure each other.

Anna flinched at the sound of a sharp step outside. Thomasin opened the door and Lady Isabel, gaunt and majestic in black, swept past her with a velvet box in her hands.

'For your wedding day, Anna,' she said abruptly. 'My father gave it to me, and I always said you'd wear it on your wedding day, so you shall.'

Anna opened the box and gasped. She drew out what looked to Thomasin like a skein of silver but was a necklace, intricately worked with twists, links and blue stones. She handed it to Thomasin and lifted her hair while Thomasin fastened it round her neck and settled it into place.

'Thomasin,' said Lady Isabel, who did not seem interested in how the necklace looked, 'a word with you alone.'

They stepped into the cool chapel. Lady Isabel unclasped a simple silver chain from her own neck and fastened it around Thomasin's.

'For you, as a token of my thanks,' she said. 'Do your best. And Thomasin…' She held her firmly by her shoulders and seemed, for the first time, to look motherly. 'If you fail, I will know you tried. Have you everything you need?'

Thomasin nodded. She had checked everything, several times over. She had laid aside the spindle that always hung at her waist, though she felt incomplete without it. She couldn't spin on Anna's wedding day. One tiny silver flask, no bigger than her thumb, was between her breasts, tightly laced under her bodice. Another lay in the tight, inner sleeve under her gown. A sheathed dagger waited in the other sleeve, and another in the hem. In two days she had changed from a maidservant with a spindle to a carrier of death. It had to be this way.

'They're nearly here, my lady!' shouted Alan, so suddenly that Thomasin and Lady Isabel jumped. In the solar chamber, Anna shuddered.

Everyone from the castle had gathered, ready to gaze, gasp and be impressed. To a ripple of bowing and curtseying Anna drifted down the stairway, her hair as fine and bright as a shaft of sunlight. She looked, they said, as if she was wearing the sky, and their hearts ached for her. 'Oh, and here's Thomasin in her ghost grey gown with a crown of summer flowers on all those curls. Fresh flowers. They'll not last in this heat.'

'Look after her, Thomasin!' they whispered, but from Thomasin's face nobody could tell whether she had heard. Alan, Will and a few old men and boys, scrubbed and shaven, waited at the door to escort them. Lady Isabel stepped into place beside Thomasin. The old priest, Father Wilfrid, whose eyes were always so watery that nobody could tell if he was weeping or not, led the way to the church. The procession passed in glorious sunlight over the drawbridge to where Jankin waited.

Falcon had ridden a pace or two behind Jankin as the bridegroom galloped downhill and clattered to a halt by the church, scattering chickens and gathering a quiet, resentful crowd who held their children tightly by the hands. They glared grimly at the broken glass of their church and its blackened stones, and back at Hawk Jankin. Hawk's jerkin, crimson and gold and stolen from a gentleman, was tight at the waist and collared at the throat, and the shirt showing beneath was of fine clean linen. His spurred boots gleamed. The red hair had been washed, trimmed and tamed; he was clean shaven, and he looked lordly. The chestnut horse, not used to its new master, had been brushed and groomed fit for royalty.

Falcon, his long wild hair washed and as gleaming as a maiden's, wore deep dark brown and stayed back. Jankin was the one who must look like a king in glory. But nobody was looking at either of them now, nor at the silent mounted men around them. Everyone turned to watch as Anna glided towards the church, a wisp of a thing between Will and Alan. Falcon stretched up in his saddle to look past her at Thomasin and leaned forward to whisper to Jankin.

'Watch that one,' he said, 'your wife's shadow.'

'Her shadow?' said Jankin, not turning as he watched the procession. 'You mean the maid?'

'Just look at her,' muttered Falcon. 'She's dangerous.'

Jankin grinned. 'I won't let her hurt you,' he said, and swung himself from the saddle to kneel at Anna's feet, kiss her hand and lead her to the church door.

Father Wilfrid gabbled through the service with so many hesitations and such stammering and mumbling that Thomasin suspected he was making mistakes on purpose so that the marriage would not prove binding; or perhaps he was just terrified. She stood very still, glancing up occasionally, as Lady Isabel did, in case a miracle was granted to them: perhaps Sir Hugh and young Hugh would come galloping down the hill with fifty armed men at their backs to strike off Jankin and Falcon's heads where they stood, and Thomasin would dart in and whisk Anna to safety until it was all over. The watching crowd sighed and cried or scowled and muttered, and Lady Isabel watched with such hatred in her eyes that she seemed to burn holes into Jankin's back.

Thomasin slipped her fingers into her sleeve and curled her fingers on the hilt. Nervousness made her legs weaken. She hadn't expected that.

I could do it now, she thought. *While they make their vows. But there are too many of his men around, and there are sure to be more where we can't see them. And could I stab through that doublet?*

Take the chance now, while you have it.

No. If I do it now and get it wrong, we'll all be massacred.

Father Wilfrid made the sign of the cross with a shaking hand. It was done. Thomasin felt she was being watched. She looked up to see Falcon, grim and unsmiling, quickly turning his eyes away from her.

There was to be no wedding breakfast at the castle. Lady Isabel did not want to seem a poor hostess, but the thought of inviting Jankin and his men to her home was too much for her. Alan had advised that the whole treacherous crew should be moved off the manor and up the hill as quickly as possible, but simple courtesies must be observed and Anna must not have a shabby wedding. As Lady Isabel scolded and criticized, wine, ale and mead were brought down from the castle, bread and meat were heaped on to trestle tables, and Jankin, too, looked ready to observe the traditions, digging his hand into a saddlebag for a fistful of small coins and flinging them into the air. A few grubby children rushed to scrabble for them, but the rest were caught and held firmly by their mothers.

'You see?' whispered Anna to Thomasin. 'There is something good in Jankin.'

'He courts the children more gently than he courted you,' Thomasin muttered back.

'Thomasin!' said Anna. 'He was harsh because he thought he had to be. He doesn't have to be now.'

Thomasin decided she might as well give up and turned impatiently to where Lady Isabel's men were trundling barrels of ale and mead from the castle to be opened. Large pewter cups had been brought as Lady Isabel had more sense than to use the silver, and Alan, sweating and huffing with the heavy barrels, selected one and filled a flagon from it.

'Wedding mead, best for the best,' he said, grinning at Thomasin. 'And that includes you, lassie. This is for the castle ladies and,' he gave a nod of contempt towards Jankin, 'him who thinks he's Lord of the Manor, King of England and Pope.' He hunted through the cups. 'There's a dented one in here that's good enough for him. And that Falcon can share his master's cup if he wants.'

Thomasin's heart pounded hard and fast against the bodice that suddenly felt too tight for breath. Sweat made her clothes cling. That was Jankin's cup and Falcon might drink from it, too. It was as if Alan knew. Perhaps he did. She held the power of life and death.

Jankin and Falcon were showing off, giving the children rides on their fine, proud horses. Nobody would notice her. She sat on the cool floor of the church porch, rubbed the sweat from her hands, and tried to breathe normally.

She knew how to kill. She had been well instructed, and didn't everyone want Jankin dead? Didn't she have Lady Isabel's blessing, and wasn't she doing this for Anna, for the village, for all of them? But she hadn't known it would feel like this.

She couldn't take a life, not even Jankin's life. How could she sit in a church doorway with the holy commandments at her back, send Jankin to hell, and make a murderer of herself? But then, didn't Sir Hugh and young Hugh set out to kill when they rode to the wars? All soldiers did, and what was so different about this? The world would be better without Jankin, and she might not have such an opportunity again.

She might go to hell for killing him, but she might already be on her way there for hating him. Did you ever get out of purgatory if you murdered someone? Even if you had a good reason? If Jankin lived, he'd only commit more murders. Her hands trembled so much that she could hardly fold them to pray.

Sweet Christ, forgive me for what I'm about to do. You know why I have to. Please pardon my sin and spare me from hell. Mary, Mother of God, pray for me. Blessed Saint Anne, pray for me.

Alan was shouting for the mead, and there was no more time to think about it. With her hand still trembling, she pulled the silver vessel from her sleeve and twisted the stopper.

'Mead!' shouted Alan. 'Where's Thomasin?'

Do it, do it, and it will all be over. I will watch him die.

Holding her breath, she poured mead into the dented cup, and, using one hand to steady the other, tipped the vial.

Thin brown liquid twirled into the mead. She picked up a bit of twig to stir it so that the colour would not show, and carefully pressed the stopper back into the empty vial, taking care not to get poison on her fingers. It would be simple to throw the vessel into a ditch later. She placed the other cups on a tray, called for a servant and, holding the poisoned vessel in both hands, stepped out into the sunshine. After the shady dark, it dazzled her.

'Take the tray to Anna and Lady Isabel,' she said. 'I'll bring this one for Jankin.'

Smiling and swaggering, Jankin pushed his way through the crowd and caught Anna's hand. Thomasin held out the cup.

'I'll take it,' called Jankin. 'It will be our wedding cup. Anna, we shall drink from the same cup!'

The cup clanged to the ground. Mead splashed onto the dry earth, splattering gowns and boots. Anna darted backwards, lifting her hem.

'I'm sorry!' gabbled Thomasin. 'I thought – my hands slipped.'

Anna leaned over to kiss her. 'It's only a cup, Thomasin,' she said. 'Alan, fetch another one. Thomasin, you're shaking!'

'Take more care, Thomasin,' said Lady Isabel, but she did not sound angry. 'You're overwrought. Take yourself out of the sun.' But she patted Thomasin gently on the shoulder as she guided her away. One of her hounds sniffed at the spilled mead, and she pushed it out of the way.

Thomasin glanced over her shoulder. The dog was sniffing the puddle again but then retreated, scampering sideways as if it were afraid.

Falcon was watching it too. He looked up suddenly, and their eyes met. Thomasin turned away.

When another cup had been filled and shared, Jankin's men began to busy themselves with saddling their horses, and Lady Isabel did not press them to stay any longer. Alan came to find Thomasin.

'You're to have your own horse,' he said, nodding at a bay pony which was standing quietly while Will settled a lady's saddle on its back. 'Jankin brought the grey for Mistress Anna and the bay pony for Lady Isabel, but she'll not have it, so you can have a mount of your own. Isn't that what you've always wanted?'

He led Thomasin to the pony, hoisted her into the saddle and handed her the reins. She looked for Anna; Jankin was lifting her onto the handsome grey mare, smoothing her gown for her and even smiling up at her. *Anyone would think he loved her.* Anna took the reins and patted the horse's neck while Jankin and Falcon led their horses to drink at the trough under the oak tree.

'Will you not listen?' insisted Falcon. 'The shadow maid didn't drop the cup until you said you'd share it with Anna.'

'Didn't I tell you,' grunted Jankin, 'that you can have her for yourself?' He tugged at the horse's girth strap. 'You sort her out! But don't come to me muttering like a toothless old witch.'

Falcon shrugged, led his horse away and mounted showily – some of the ladies would be watching, even if they pretended not to. If Jankin didn't want to be warned of what that girl was up to, so be it, but he'd remember his insult. For himself, he'd keep an eye on the little dark shadow. He looked to see her turning her pony's head, taking her place beside Anna, leaning over to whisper something to her and briefly laying her fingers over Anna's hand. The lassie was up to something. He found he admired her for it.

In time Thomasin would have to be separated from Anna, because Anna would have no fight in her without her shadow. He and Jankin had an arrangement – the mistress for Hawk, the maid for Falcon. If Thomasin had to be tamed, thwarted and even broken, he would be the one to do it.

There was a last quiet fluttering around Anna. Hugs were exchanged. Tears were dried on sleeves and aprons, then hooves clattered and harnesses jingled. The grey tossed her head and the pony plodded steadily at her side as Jankin and Anna, Falcon and Thomasin rode away uphill with Jankin's men ahead and behind. At the grey rock, just past the hill's foot, Anna and Thomasin raised their hands as Lady Isabel raised hers – then Anna folded her lips very tightly and looked down as if she wanted to shield her eyes from the westering sun. They did not look back again. Thomasin pulled the wilted garland from her head, scowling as the tough stalks snagged in her hair, and tossed it into the bracken.

Anna comforted herself with thoughts of peace. Slowly, fed by her love and patience, Jankin and all about him would be transformed. And Thomasin reminded herself that she still had two daggers, a vial of poison and a mind set to kill. The paths grew steeper, craggier and further, further, further from their home.

Chapter Five

The sun was low, and Thomasin was glad of it. She had brought lavender and rose water to stroke into Anna's temples in case of headaches, and her own head was tight with heat. Even Anna no longer looked her best, her face frowning and drawn with sun and tiredness, her hair tangled and in need of a brush.

'I'll tell them to stop,' Thomasin whispered. 'You need a rest.'

'We may as well get there,' said Anna. 'It can't be that much further, surely? Isn't that it?'

Beyond huddles of trees and craggy, uneven ground, the battlemented top of a dark grey tower reared up. The ground suddenly became steeper and rockier, so Thomasin gathered up the reins more tightly, pulling up the pony's head, and saw Anna do the same. Jankin twisted in the saddle and grinned.

'Your horses know the ground!' he called. As the first full view of High Crag Tower came into sight, Thomasin felt Anna's heart fall to her stomach and turn, as her own did.

'I'll look after you,' she whispered. 'I won't leave you.' And in her heart, she made a promise – *I will get you out of that place*.

The tower rose before them like the giant in a story. Tiny windows spied out at them.

'How is there room for everyone?' whispered Anna.

Jankin laughed, and Thomasin glared at him. The question had been meant for her.

'You're not used to us,' he said. 'And we're not used to ladies.' He jumped from the saddle. 'We've made what space we can for you.'

Thomasin did not wait to be lifted from her pony. She dismounted with a wriggle and a jump as Jankin gently lifted Anna down and led her to the tower. Its shadow fell on them. A man running ahead opened a door, and as its darkness swallowed Anna, Thomasin hurried behind her so that it should swallow her too. In the sudden gloom where she could see nothing, there was a smell of burned peat and heather, sweat, stale hay, leather and earth.

'The men gather and sleep here,' said Jankin. 'We bring the animals in when we must. And here…'

Thomasin could see better now. There were blankets and swords, bows and arrows neatly stacked as if they were supplies in a store room. The hearth was messy and unswept, with a heap of logs beside it. Jankin, his boots creaking, crossed the floor to a small door, lifted the bolt, and with a sweep of his arm summoned them to follow him.

The door opened to a spiral staircase so dark and uneven that Thomasin climbed with one hand on the wall and the other lifting both her own hem and Anna's. It was partly to keep them from tripping up, but also to avoid the dust and dirt that she was sure must lie on the steps, though she couldn't see any. She could feel Falcon's presence at her back. *Let him. Something to land on if I fall, and if he touches me he's near enough to kill.* He was watching her. If she even felt her sleeve to make sure she could reach her dagger, he would notice. She wished he had stayed where she could see him.

Falcon was staying close enough to keep Thomasin from

running away and far enough back to defend himself if she drew a knife. He'd seen no sign of one, but he was sure she was armed. She had that look. He had old scars earned by a look like that. He watched her hands, but she seemed so hampered with yards of her own gown and Anna's – good God, why did small women need such huge clothes? – that she couldn't try anything dangerous just yet. And she'd not do anything that would put Anna at risk. Step by step, he followed her. Step by step, he mistrusted her.

A door clanked. Jankin led them into a very small, square and surprisingly clean chamber.

'My lady,' he said, 'pardon my poor house. It is not fit to receive ladies, but we have done what we can.'

Thomasin glanced quickly round the room. It seemed to be made even smaller by the closed door, and Falcon standing with his back to it. A torch flared on the wall, and candles stood on a small, dark wooden chest. There was a wide fireplace where a fire had been laid but not lit and two narrow windows with broken glass panes. The floor showed a thin layer of something like grain husk – this must have been used as a store room – and the boxes she and Anna had brought with them had already been heaped in a corner. Threadbare tapestries hung on two walls, too faded for the pictures to be recognizable at all, and a straw mattress lay in one corner. By the fireplace stood a padded stool topped with black velvet, the only elegant piece of furniture in the room. It must have been stolen.

Thomasin had worked and played in a castle long enough to know what tight, awkward places spiral staircases were. Until now the only door she had seen had been the door to that staircase, and the leaded windows were tiny. If they needed to escape quickly, they couldn't do it from here.

'This has been a store room,' Jankin was saying. 'We have done what we could.' He swept aside a tapestry with a flurry of dust that made Anna cough, but Thomasin's eyes brightened when she saw there was a door behind the tapestry. Jankin was heaving it open and showing them into the next room, a simple chamber with a chest, a stained and scratched table, and a large plain bed which seemed to draw all eyes towards it. Two men already in the chamber looked at each other, winked and muttered something that made them laugh so that Anna blushed and looked at the floor. Thomasin silenced them with a glare, but she knew they were grinning as Falcon led them back into the tiny square chamber.

Still, what she had seen was useful. The windows were bigger in that room, and there was something on the floor which looked like a trapdoor. Jankin replaced the tapestry and Thomasin gestured Anna towards the velvet topped stool.

'The maid will sleep in this room tonight,' said Jankin. 'And you will both rest here at present.' He shouted a command, and from the bedchamber came a man bearing pewter cups and a jug, followed by the other with bread, meat and cheese. They set out the meal on the chest, found there wasn't enough room, and put the jug and cups by the fireplace.

Thomasin hadn't been sure what to expect at High Crag Tower. In her worst imaginings, she had been shut up in a cold damp cell away from Anna while Anna screamed for her help. This awkward attempt at courtesy, with the men offering something that was half a bow and half a nod, and Jankin pouring the wine himself, puzzled and unsettled her. She wished he'd just go, but he was speaking to them as he handed Anna her cup.

'Not so long ago,' he said, 'Hollylaw and all its lands

44

belonged to my family. After the reign of the last King Richard it was taken from us and handed to – remind us, Falcon…'

'… a bunch of lilies,' said Falcon without a trace of a smile.

'The Lillie family hold my family's right to this day,' went on Jankin, 'whichever kings have come and gone since then. Lancaster and York make no difference; neither of them have returned our lands to us.' He placed a cup before Anna, and as she reached for it his fingers curled over hers.

'Is that justice?' he asked. 'Is it, Anna? Our birthright, the lands we had held and cared for for centuries? That castle was my family's home, and they were thrown from it. Is that justice?'

'It is hard,' admitted Anna softly, 'but you only held the land under the king, and –'

'… and what happens now,' he demanded, 'when nobody knows who's the king and who's the traitor?' Thomasin saw his hand tighten.

'But,' said Anna, ' it isn't the fault of my family or the people that…'

No longer listening, he let go of Anna's hand. 'What could I do?' He didn't wait for an answer. 'Take it by force, or marry it, or both. One way or the other, Anna, you'll be back at Hollylaw.' He frowned down at Thomasin. 'What's the matter?'

Thomasin, examining Anna's hand, scowled up at him.

'You've hurt her,' she said.

'Shall I take the shadow away, Hawk?' offered Falcon. Thomasin pressed closer to Anna, putting both her hands round Anna's hurt one.

'Patience, Falcon, you can take your pleasure later,' said Jankin. 'Now, listen to me, both of you. For the present, you will stay here. We have vital matters to attend to.'

Vital matters that we are not to know about, thought Thomasin. *And if Falcon tries to take his pleasure with* me, *he won't live to regret it for long*. She caught the look that passed between Jankin and Falcon, which seemed like a shaft of dark through daylight. She let go of Anna's hand and slipped her right hand to her left wrist.

'There is food and drink for you here,' went on Jankin. 'Thomasin, if your mistress is cold, light the fire. Unpack her boxes. Take care of her. Anna, urgent work will keep me away late tonight, but I will come to you.' He bowed abruptly to Anna, then he and Falcon were gone so quickly that the dagger was only half out of Thomasin's sleeve. She kicked the door in frustration.

'Take care of her!' she cried. 'What does he think I always do?'

She could have done it. Falcon, then the same dagger for Jankin – but Jankin would have had time to overpower her. She'd have to wait for a moment when Jankin was alone, and surely Falcon wouldn't follow him to the bridal bed?

A chamber like this – dense-walled with few windows – would soon grow cold. She opened a box and drew out a warm mantle because she felt better if she had ordinary things to do: shaking out Anna's clothes, setting out her comb and the bottle of rose water.

'Let me help,' said Anna, and Thomasin didn't try to stop her, knowing that she, too, needed to be occupied. 'We can move some of these into the bedch… the other chamber.'

Thomasin pushed aside the tapestry and tried the door. It did not move. She shook it, put her shoulder to it and pushed.

'Bolted,' she said. She examined the locks, and kicked it. 'Locked and bolted against us. You have a fine bridegroom. He'll be back soon, or somebody will, and we can go through.'

Anna giggled nervously. 'Perhaps he's decorating it for me. Greenery and flowers.'

'And flagons of mead,' said Thomasin, and their laughter became wild and infectious, a rocking, tearful laughter that terrified Thomasin even as she went on laughing, because it was laughter masking the fear, harsh laughter that knew there would be no mead or flowers for Anna's wedding night but only darkness in a rough bed. If they laughed loudly enough they would drown out their fear. Thomasin wiped tears from her eyes and poured more wine for Anna. She wouldn't normally dream of giving Anna too much to drink, but tonight it might make it easier for her.

She unpacked Anna's belongings and, underneath the cloaks and linen, found the spindle she had forgotten about. With its half spun fleece, it was a piece of her home. She hugged it for a moment, then felt ashamed because she was behaving like a child with a doll, not a young woman with enemies to kill. She turned the spindle and teased out the thread. With the comfortable old shape of the spindle in her hands she twisted, twirled and turned it, and wished that this were over.

It will all be over soon. We shall be safely back at the castle, and they will never trouble us again. But loneliness wrapped her like icy water, cutting her off from Anna, who must not know anything until the killing was done. The voice still niggled underneath like a fault through a piece of sewing – *you can't do it.* It was one thing to plunge a knife into the heart of a beast, but a man? *You'll fail. When it comes to the point, wench, you won't do it. Haven't you had your chances already? When WILL you do it?*

I will do it, she told herself, *and I just won't let myself think about it. I have two daggers and a bottle of poison in my clothes, and how long can I carry all that around without Anna knowing?*

Anna was speaking in a voice so low that Thomasin had hardly noticed.

'Beg pardon?' she asked. Softly, uneasily, Anna said it again.

'Tonight – do you think it will hurt?'

Thomasin stopped turning the spindle and hugged her. 'Maybe just the first time,' she said. She had heard all sorts of talk among the servants about marriage beds and had made up her own mind about how much of it might be true. Apparently every poor unmarried peasant girl who gave birth to a red-haired baby said it was Jankin's, just as every brown-eyed baby was blamed on Falcon. It wouldn't help to say so, but at least Anna would be going to bed with a man who knew what to do. 'It might just hurt a bit the first time,' she repeated.

'That's what mother told me,' said Anna, as if she hadn't been sure whether to believe her until now. She looked without interest at the hairbrush and smock Thomasin had laid out, and said, 'Will the candles be lit?'

'Do you want them lit?'

'Oh, yes!' said Anna earnestly, then looked down at her hands. Her cheeks were deep pink. 'I think so. I mean, I don't like the idea of it all happening in the dark. But then I'd have to see him and he'd have to see me, and I think I'd rather neither...' She giggled, but the giggle was high and almost like tears. 'I'd rather neither of us could see anything!'

Thomasin squeezed her hand and hated Jankin. *She's terrified*, she thought. *No decent husband would insist on bedding her tonight, not while she's still so scared, but he's no decent husband.* Restlessly, she got up to peer down from the narrow window.

'He's taking long enough,' she said. She turned away and wriggled crossly, trying not to fidget. 'Shall we sing something?' But Anna's voice was tight, cracking on the high notes, and there was no point in going on. Again, Thomasin stamped to the tiny window.

Every man in Hollylaw wanted to kill Jankin. *So why do I have to do it? Why couldn't one of his own men have killed him in a drunken fight, why couldn't his horse have stumbled and thrown him to his death? Even now, dear God, couldn't Jankin's guardian angel look the other way long enough for him to choke, or fall, or quarrel with Falcon so that Falcon kills him, and I won't have to? Falcon's as bad as Jankin – one more killing wouldn't matter to him. Why should I have to do it?*

I can't.

I must. I have no choice. She felt again for the dagger in her sleeve. *Why can't he just walk through that door now, and I'll get it done? And why did I ever think I could kill both of them, Jankin and Falcon, and get Anna safely out?*

'Thomasin, be calm!' implored Anna. 'You're all fidgety, and you make me nervous.'

'I'm sorry,' said Thomasin. 'But your husband should be back. It's getting cool now. I can't even put your things in your proper chamber, if that's what he thinks it is.'

'Sh!' said Anna. Thomasin listened. The low mumble of voices came from the next room. 'Somebody's there. They'll come and open the door soon.'

Thomasin pressed her ear to the door frame and then to the keyhole, but nothing could be heard clearly. When boots sounded on the floor she sprang back, but still nobody came.

'They think this is still a house without a mistress,' she snapped. 'Time they learned.' She banged her fist on the door, waited for an answer, and tried again. The voices stopped, but nobody came to the door. Thomasin banged harder, then snatched the poker, hammered with that, and went on hammering until the door jerked open and she stumbled. A large, dark complexioned man with a stubbled chin stood with one hand on the door and the other on the doorpost, barring her way. Thomasin remembered Falcon barking orders at this man earlier in the day, and calling him 'Clem'.

'Clem, my lady has been kept in here too long,' she said, with the poker still in her hand. 'I wish to move her things to her bridal chamber.'

There was a loud laugh from inside the room.

'Bridal chamber!' said a rough voice. 'That's good.'

'You're to stay here,' said Clem. 'Hawk's orders.'

Thomasin stood firm and tilted up her chin. 'When will he be back?'

The rough laughter came again. A red-haired man with a scarred face shambled to the door. 'Depends how long it takes him…' began the red-haired man, but Clem wouldn't let him finish.

'Shut your mouth, Nick,' ordered Clem. 'You ladies are to stay here. You want wine, food, you call me. You want your men, you'll have to wait.' He tried to peer past Thomasin at Anna, though Thomasin did her best to screen her. 'Be patient, Flower,' he called. 'He'll be back tonight for you.'

Thomasin slammed the door hard in his face, and immediately regretted it. She had just thrown away her chance of asking him more questions and getting a good look at as much of the tower as possible. She battered at the door with the poker. 'I must speak!'

'Patience is a fine thing, madam!' called back Clem with a grin in his voice, but this time his voice came from further away. A trapdoor clattered.

'And if you need a pisspot,' called Clem, 'there's one by the…'

Thomasin had already found the earthenware pot. She picked it up and would have hurled it at the door if Anna hadn't stopped her.

'We'll need that,' she said. 'We wouldn't want to…'

'Sh!' said Thomasin. 'Quiet, Anna!' She shut her eyes to help herself concentrate, pressed her ear as near as she could to the window, and listened.

'Harness,' she said, 'and horses. It sounds as if they're gathering for a ride.'

'Tonight?' exclaimed Anna. 'Where would they –'

She met Thomasin's eyes, and did not finish. There was no need to tell each other where Jankin might lead his men tonight.

'We need to find out exactly what's happening,' said Thomasin. She knelt at the locked and bolted door to the next chamber, using her knife to tease at the lock and wriggle the bolts. It did no good. The bolts were too strong and too many. The other door was guarded, and there would be more guards at the foot of the stair. She glanced round the room, unlacing her skirt from her bodice as she did, feeling better now that she had something to do.

'All those years,' she said, tugging at the lacing, 'all the time we spent climbing up and down backstairs and dangling each other out of windows. Jankin needn't think he can keep us in.'

'But there isn't a window…' began Anna.

Thomasin smiled brightly. 'There's a chimney!' she said. She laid aside the gown and stood in her bodice and a smock that reached just to her knees.

'You can't climb a chimney!' cried Anna.

'Sh!' said Thomasin. 'I couldn't last time I tried, but I'm

taller now. That chimney's wide enough for them to smoke stolen venison in it. I should think they all connect, so I can get from this chimney into the next room and open the door.'

'You'll get filthy!'

'Of course I will! That's why I took my gown off. I'll leave my bodice on. Give me a push.'

She braced herself against the sides of the chimney breast, took a deep breath, scrabbled for foot and hand holds, and, with a heave from Anna, launched herself up. *Holy Saint Anne, girl, of course it's dark – what do you expect? It's a chimney! Don't think about the dark.* The cold made her gasp, and she breathed in soot and darkness. *Reach for the next hand hold. The next toe hold.* She pressed her back hard against the rough, cold stone, feeling her way up, scraping and clutching. When her right hand found nothing and flailed in the air she shrieked and bit her lip. Anna's anxious voice reached her from far away.

'No harm done,' she called back, though the soot roughened her voice and made her cough. 'I think the chimney links with the other one here, if I can get into it.'

She'd have to turn round, bracing her hands and feet until she faced the other way. *As if it weren't hard enough.* It might become too narrow, it might be too tight to get out, but it was the only thing to try.

The air became thicker, dusty and suffocating; the urgency to breathe clean air drove her on. Shuffling, feeling her way, she reached the dark passage which, she supposed, linked the fireplaces of the two chambers. There was just room to crawl on hands and knees. She stifled her coughs, pulled away the cobwebs that trailed across her face, and squeezed her eyes shut until dim light came from the empty fireplace beneath her.

Climbing down proved harder than climbing up. In the dark she slipped; dropping into the hearth with a shower of cold ash, she smothered a yelp as the rough stones sheared at her leg. Whitened logs spilled into dust. She pulled hair from her mouth, gulped down the air, ran to the door and wrenched the bolts.

'Thomasin!' cried Anna. Thomasin stood in the doorway, filthy with soot, her smock torn and cobwebs and dust in her hair. There were white tracks down her face where soot and coughing had made her eyes water and smudged the dirt. Dead and living spiders hung from her curls. Soot mingled with dark blood on her grazed legs, and a thin line of blood trickled to her ankle. Anna shrank back. Then she reached out to hug her.

'Not in that gown, you don't,' ordered Thomasin, and ushered her into the chamber where now the messy fireplace was what mattered, not the bed. 'Come in here. If we hear anyone coming, we'll fly back into the small room.'

'But Jankin will see…' began Anna.

'Leave him to me,' said Thomasin grimly. 'I'll talk my way out of this, and I'll say it was nothing to do with you. Listen!'

From this room, with its larger windows, the sound of voices was clearer. They took up places at either side of the window, their backs flat against the wall, their faces turned to hear all they could. A ringing clang made them jump with terror, but all voices stopped except Jankin's.

'Tonight,' he was saying, 'I will take back what is mine. They will not be expecting visitors.' There was a rumble of laughter. 'They will expect me to have more important things to do tonight. Anna is mine. Tonight, we walk into Hollylaw. Kill anyone who dares oppose you. Alan the Steward and Will the Smith must die. Leave Lady Isabel to me – for the moment I shall keep her under lock and key. And when I take Anna back to Hollylaw, you will remember that I am Lord of the Manor now, and she is my Lady.'

From the crowd, a voice mumbled something that Anna and Thomasin couldn't clearly hear. They heard laughter, and Falcon's answer.

'Don't concern yourselves,' he said. 'Sir Hugh and his son will not come back from the war.'

Anger turned Thomasin's stomach and weakened her legs. She looked across the window at Anna, who was so pale that she looked ready to faint or be sick. Thomasin's fingers were clenched. *Sir Hugh and his son will not come back from the war.* He would take Hollylaw that night and bring Anna home to it in the morning, knowing that no Lord of Hollylaw would ever return to challenge him. Thomasin no longer had any doubts about whether she could kill. She wished she had poison and weaponry enough for the whole crew of them.

'Ride in silence,' Jankin was ordering. 'I'll have no clanking swords tonight. Take torches and flints, but show no light between the brow of the hill and the edge of the village, when we light the torches for the fiery ride and scare their guts into the ground. But spare the villeins who don't stand up to you. We'll need them. Once we're in our rightful places, we'll show them who's their master now.'

Anna and Thomasin looked into each other's eyes across the window.

'Can we get there on foot before they get there on horseback?' suggested Thomasin.

'Couldn't we take our own horses?' said Anna.

'They'd need saddling first,' said Thomasin. 'And we'd be more conspicuous on horses. We'd have to find a way through the trees, and it might be slower than the way they're going.'

'We'll go on foot, then,' said Anna. She sank to her knees, crawled from the window to keep from being seen, and rubbed her hands in the ashes of the fireplace.

'What are you doing?' whispered Thomasin.

'Getting as dirty as you,' Anna whispered back. 'Then we're less likely to be seen.'

Thomasin, too, crawled away from the window. She found her discarded gown and laced it back on.

'It's better if only one of us goes,' she said. 'It'll be hard enough to get away without being seen. Two are easier to see than one.'

'And harder to catch,' said Anna. She took off the pearl cap and ruffled soot into her hair. Thomasin tried not to wince. This was no time to think about Anna's appearance, but it was such a shame about her hair and that beautiful gown.

'Fasten my hair up, Thomasin,' said Anna. Standing on the trapdoor in case anybody tried to come in, Thomasin twisted and pinned the hair that was now thick with dirt, trying to work out how to take the greatest risks herself without Anna realizing it.

'We don't have to leave together,' she said. 'It might be better if one of us stays behind to let the other one get away.'

'And then go by a different route,' said Anna.

'And if any of Jankin's men come back while the second of us is still here, she can cover up for the first. Say she's asleep or something. And explain the hearth. We'll have to say a bird flew down the chimney.'

'So where has it gone?' asked Anna, and they both said together, 'back up the other chimney,' and laughed, pressing their hands to their mouths to stifle the laughter that was not right, not now.

'Stand still, or I'll never get this done,' said Thomasin. If she went first and was seen, they would chase her, giving Anna a chance to get away. 'I'll go first. We don't know how we're going to get out yet, but the trapdoor must lead down to that room where the men sleep. We'd have to be sure it's empty before the first of us climbs down.'

'Thomasin,' said Anna, and Thomasin took a step back and gave a brief nod, because this was Anna's voice for giving orders. 'It's more dangerous to go first. I'll do it.'

'I'm here to look after you,' said Thomasin. She tucked up her skirt so it wouldn't encumber her. 'Lady Isabel gave me orders to do that, and I have to obey her orders, my lady. That means I go first.'

'We're not in my mother's house!' ordered Anna sharply. 'This is my husband's tower, so I'm the mistress here. And it's my family's manor we're fighting for.'

'Please, Anna,' begged Thomasin, 'we don't have time to…'

'… argue,' said Anna. 'No, we don't. Where's the dice?'

Thomasin had laid them on the black velvet stool when she unpacked. She placed them in Anna's hand.

'Highest number,' said Anna. She threw the dice. Thomasin threw them. Then they exchanged necklaces and hugged each other very tightly, in case they never met again.

Chapter Six

As dusk closed in, the horses picked their way down a hill they knew well. Nobody spoke. On the dry ground a twig snapped, sharp as the crack of a whip in the quiet. Darkness was around them, stars above them. It was a riding of ghosts until the lights of the castle were in sight.

At the tower, a dog in the doorway stretched, crept forwards and growled deep in his throat. Then, barking like the breaking of rocks, he sprang into the dark, and every hound in the tower ran to join him.

Clem and Nick were no longer able to ride, which made them the ragdoll of everyone else's jokes. Already today they had endured the rest of the men calling them 'ladies' maids', and those two lasses had been more trouble than they were worth. But they could still run, and run they did, to find out what the noise was about. The hounds were tugging at a cloak as the wearer pulled it off and stumbled on without it – but they were too fast for her, snapping and dragging at her gown.

'Bring her down!' ordered Clem, but the hounds had already dragged her to the ground. 'Nick, get her inside.'

Jankin reined in his horse and held out his arm. The men slowed and stopped. Jankin advanced slowly, Falcon keeping pace with him.

'They're gey busy tonight,' remarked Falcon. Jankin leaned

forward in the saddle and pointed.

Figures on the drawbridge held torches. Archers stood on the battlements, with more running to join them.

'Plagues of deepest hell!' exclaimed Falcon. 'How did they know?'

Jankin pointed again. This time, Falcon saw a small figure in a plain cloak, running among the defenders.

'Thomasin!' he said. 'How did she get out? I'll take a knife to Clem and Nick.'

'We should have knifed that creeping shadow witch spawn before we got as far as the tower,' muttered Jankin. 'I only let her live to keep the other one sweet.'

Falcon waited. He felt Jankin's rage as if it vibrated in the air, snarling and growling and gathering itself to spring, rage against Hollylaw, against Anna and Thomasin, against Falcon himself for being right about Thomasin, of the hunter as the prey is snatched away. He shrugged.

'They're only old men and boys, Hawk,' he said. 'Women and peasants.' Jankin did not appear to hear him as he turned in the saddle to address the men.

'We're betrayed,' he shouted, and a murmur of anger ran through the men. 'My lady's kitchen cat has escaped. When I give the order, ride hard! Take the castle! If the drawbridge is up, use ropes, do anything, but take it. Spare not one life, no man, woman, child, except for one. Spare Thomasin! I promise a reward to anyone who brings her to me, and *I* shall not spare her! Ready! For the Hawk! For High Crag Tower!'

'For Hawk! For High Crag Tower!' Torches were lit, flames blazed upwards like the leaping of demons, and the last of the fiery rides poured down in fury on Hollylaw.

Those who lived furthest from the castle were cut down as they tried to run, their houses hacked, firehooks, ploughs and tables wrenched out and wrecked to be lashed together and used as grappling irons to make a crossing for the moat. Take the castle! The drawbridge was up. Bridge the moat, swim it, swim the horses, take the castle! From the battlements, arrows and rocks hurtled down. Alan the Steward and Will the Smith bellowed, roared and swore, and the high clear voice of Lady Isabel screamed out orders. Men, women and children shrieked, cried, cursed; men, women and children fell as Jankin's men rode through blood. Arrows swooped, grappling irons flew, men and horses swam, a makeshift bridge was hauled over bodies into place. Pierced and blood-spattered bodies splashed into the moat. Horses screamed with terror. Mothers, crying out and dying, fell on the bodies of their children. Blood was smeared over cattle, walls and faces, and soaked into the parched ground. Animals bleated, stamped, squawked.

'Spare the beasts!' yelled Jankin as he plunged his sword into the side of the man seizing his horse's bridle. 'We need them!'

'Hollylaw for the Hawk!' cried Falcon, and leapt for a rope anchored to the castle wall. Alan stretched down from the battlements to slice through it, but a rush of arrows from Jankin's crew sent him to his knees and Falcon kicked his way up the wall.

'Drawbridge!' he shouted, watching all the time for a grey-cloaked figure. Will the Smith fell at the drawbridge, choking on his own blood, dead before Jankin's men trampled over him as Jankin cried out for victory and for Thomasin.

How did the fire in the castle start? Jankin's men carried torches. One spark would have been enough to set the stairway tapestries alight. With the village in flames behind them and the stairs in flames below, Jankin and Falcon hacked and cursed their way through the keep, slashing down the tapestries to keep the fire from spreading. Men who came at them fell with sword wounds in their heads and hearts, the air grew thick with blood and smoke, and the floors grew slippery. Screams, as fierce and terrible as the cries of tormented souls, came from beneath them. With swords stained and dripping, Jankin and Falcon stood at last in the solar chamber, sweating and swearing, looking down at the crowning of flame over all the village.

'Hollylaw is mine,' said Jankin. 'Bring me Thomasin!'

The fire on the stairs still smouldered, and a beam had caught light and fallen. They turned over every corpse they found, some still hot and in ashes, some disfigured, many in grey cloaks like Thomasin's. They did not find her. The upper rooms were charred and smoked, but had not caught fire. Jankin sat down on the chair at the head of the solar chamber.

'Tell them to go on searching until they find her,' he said. 'And I'll go back to the tower to give my wife the attention she desires.' He turned sharply, and raised his voice. 'Has nobody found that hell's witch?'

'Sir,' said one of the men, 'there's that many dead, and half of them you couldn't put a name to. Their own mothers wouldn't know them.'

'She's got away,' muttered Jankin.

'We would have seen her,' said Falcon. 'The men would have seen her. She'll be in among the bodies, it's just a matter of finding which one's hers.' He glared at the huddle of men in the doorway. 'Look again.'

'Anna will be all mine now,' said Jankin. 'Is there no wine in this castle? Find me wine. Now Anna won't have her hellcat to hide her and poison her mind against me.'

Falcon found a jug of wine on a side table and poured it.

He no longer had to watch Thomasin, fierce, dangerous Thomasin, but the knowledge that he had been right about her hung uneasily between himself and Jankin. And something else niggled round his heart like a rough edge.

'Anna must have helped her,' growled Jankin. 'At least, she didn't stop her, did she?' He banged his fist on the table. 'Back to the tower!'

Jankin and Falcon rode side by side up the hill until High Crag Tower came into sight against a sullen sky. They strode in, stained with blood and smoke, their faces grim.

'Is she here?' roared Jankin.

'Yes, Hawk,' barked Clem. 'She tried –'

'Shut your mouth.' He stamped up to the chamber. 'ANNA!'

'Sir,' began Clem, but Jankin pushed him aside, held out a blackened hand for the keys, threw open the door, and stood still.

'What have you done?' screamed Thomasin.

It was only a second but it was a second that would return, over and again, in nightmares, in unwanted flashes of memory, hellish in torchlight. Time after time after time, Jankin would see this – Thomasin, wild-eyed, soot-streaked and staring, wrapped for warmth in Anna's cloak. Time after time after time, Thomasin would see Jankin with Falcon at his shoulder, both bloodied and dirty, reeking of slaughter and smoke, and the terrifying fury on Jankin's face.

'Where's Anna?' she demanded, looking from one to the other. 'Tell me!'

Jankin's face twitched with rage. Thomasin read their faces. Blood. Silence. Horror. She understood. With the dagger in her hand, she sprang for Jankin's throat.

Jankin caught her wrist as the dagger point touched him and with one twist forced it from her grip but she was clawing his face, kicking him off balance so that he fell to the floor. She fought to catch his neck – but Falcon was dragging her back as she thrashed, clawed and screamed in his arms. One arm was round her waist pinioning her arms, the other twisted in her hair as she tried to bite him. 'Give me some help here!' he yelled over her screams.

Nick and Clem ran in. 'She has the power of all hell in her. Get her feet. Put her on the floor. Are there any more weapons here?'

She twisted and wriggled all she could, squeezing her eyes shut against hot tears of humiliation as Falcon patted briskly at her bodice, sleeves and skirt. She hated him. *Why is there need for hell and its demons when you walk the earth?* She raised her head to bite, but Nick forced it down again and she roared with fury.

'Shut it, wench,' ordered Nick.

'Keep her still, can't you?' muttered Falcon. 'There's a rent in her skirt where a dagger might have been. Where is it now, girl?'

'I gave it to Anna,' snarled Thomasin, and Anna's name made her throat lurch. 'I wish she'd left it in your heart. And I wish she'd killed the hell hawk first.'

'She's got silver in here too,' said Falcon. Coins clattered to the floor. 'Did you think you could bribe your way out?'

Jankin was on his feet. 'Put her against the wall,' he ordered. Thomasin's back was pushed roughly to the wall. Torchlight brought Jankin's face nearer, and she spat. Whatever they did to her, they'd pay for it. When he pushed his face close to hers, she flinched.

'I did right by Hollylaw,' he growled. 'I could have carried off the lass by force, but I married her. I was ready to take the castle tonight, with as little bloodshed as might be. Tomorrow, we would have ridden down together, my wife at my side, you following after. Anna and I would have taken our rightful places as lord and lady, you would have cared for her as before, and all would have been as it should. Because they were warned, the castle and the village fought me. What did they get? Fire and sword. All of them! It was your idea, wasn't it? You, girl, you have sent the Flower of Hollylaw to her death, and all of them with her. Do you understand?' He grasped her chin in his hands, forced her face upwards, and hammered the words like nails. 'There… is… no… Anna. Have you understood that? She's dead!'

Thomasin was shuddering. She pressed her lips tightly and fought the working of her face, but it was no good. Hot tears overwhelmed her. Hating herself, she lowered her head and sobbed, but Jankin was forcing her face up again.

'Why did she wear your cloak?'

'I made her,' she whispered. 'Hers was too conspicuous.'

'And you sent her,' said Jankin. 'If someone had to go and die, why wasn't it you? What sort of a servant are you?'

'We had to warn them,' she said, and broke into more sobs as the events of a few hours ago came back to her – only a few irreversible hours ago, when Anna had been alive. 'We both went. Different ways. I wanted to go first, and she argued, so we threw the dice.'

He hit her across the face with such force that the men holding her flinched. 'You'll hang in the morning,' he said. 'Slowly, from the tower. No, from Hollylaw Castle, so you can see what you've done.'

'Hawk,' said Falcon, and with a jerk of his head drew Jankin away to the shadows. More men had come into the room now, and someone took Falcon's place in holding Thomasin against the wall.

'You gave her to me,' said Falcon.

Jankin shrugged. 'Then you can hang her.'

'She's no use to me hanged,' said Falcon.

Jankin grinned unpleasantly. 'Just because she cried,' he sneered. Falcon did not reply. He held Hawk's gaze.

Could anyone but Falcon have got away with it? The men holding Thomasin took their eyes from her, watched the two men, then glanced at each other. Jankin gave something like a jerk and a shrug.

'Leave her here,' Falcon ordered the men. He shouted down the trapdoor, 'Two of you, get up here and take over from these two limp-brained lassies. Guard this girl – and this time, guard her well.'

By the torchlight, he looked more closely at Thomasin. He put out a hand and touched her neck, though she pressed away from him and set her teeth.

'That's Anna's jewel,' he said.

'We exchanged them,' she spat at him. 'You wouldn't understand.'

The door banged as Falcon and Jankin left. The lock fell with a clatter. Light was beginning to rise in the sky; a fiery, angry light glaring beyond the slit windows. Thomasin fell to her hands and knees, struggling to breathe. Anna was dead. Hollylaw was destroyed. Lady Isabel, Will, Alan. All gone. She curled up tightly, hugging herself. If she had not looked for a way to escape, this would not have happened. If she had insisted on going first, it might still have happened, but Anna would have lived. But then Anna would be the one still here, among Jankin's crew, with not a friend left alive. Dry sobs lurched her. Nothing existed for her in the world except this place, these men and the unbearable guilt.

She searched inside herself for something to give her strength. She found anger and hatred and tried to scream, but could not, so she hurled the water jug at the door. The plate was next, then her shoes; the power of hurling and breaking, the destruction, the crash and clang and shatter only assuaged the pain a little, so she picked up the broken fragments, threw them again, and smashed the tiny windows with her fists so that blood ran down her arms. When she had nothing left except Anna's gown and Anna's soft indoor shoes and hairbrushes she would not throw those, so she threw herself, violently and furiously, against the door, again and again, pounding it and kicking until she was too exhausted to go on. She took Anna's hairbrush from the chest, wrapped herself in Anna's cloak, and curled up on the floor, shaking, clutching the hairbrush.

Falcon, Jankin and a dozen of the men rode again the way they had come, down to the village and the castle, smelling the burning long before they saw the devastation. The survivors had fled. Charred, roofless walls of wattle and daub gave way to charcoal shreds of tables and blackened cooking pots. A few chickens squawked and scratched in the ashes. Pigs rooted about. Charred, twisted shapes lay on the ground.

'Clear the bodies,' ordered Jankin. 'Dig a pit.'

One at a time they rode over the drawbridge, cautiously, in case it had weakened and might give way. The morning sun pretended that it was a fair day, but a child's body floated past in the moat and Jankin's men cast dour glances between them.

The castle's west-facing front had suffered most. The windows had blown out, and scorched scraps of ruined hangings dangled. Jankin, Falcon and their followers dismounted and picked their way over bodies.

It was far worse in daylight. Huge and brutal, the collapsed roof beam lay across the stairs, holding down black-grimed bodies. Their clothes were crumbling into grey flakes, their charred fingers were outstretched. From the remnants of a headdress and a robe they recognized Lady Isabel, a sword still in her jewelled hand. Some of the dead still had faces, some had not, and it was hard to know which was worse. Hardened fighters turned away to vomit.

'Get them moved,' ordered Jankin. The beam splintered and crumbled into charcoal as they heaved it out of the way. With the toe of his boot Jankin pushed over one body, then another, looking without expression at what might have been a cook, what might have been a serving girl, what must have been a child.

'Falcon,' he muttered.

Close to the body of Lady Isabel lay a girl. Jankin had looked for a gleam of Anna's golden hair, but this girl's hair had been burned away, and her face… he did not look for long at what remained of her face. A few fragments of fabric still clung round her. Shreds of grey cloak were recognizable, and he lifted one on his sword.

'They all wore cloaks like that,' said Falcon, and stooped to pick up a blackened coin lying on the ground. He rubbed it on his sleeve.

'Silver,' he said. 'Thomasin had these stitched into her clothes. Daresay they both did the same.'

Jankin bent closer, then darted to look at the dagger in the burned hand.

'See this, Falcon?' Falcon squatted down to look. 'Same as Thomasin's.'

Jankin did not like to touch the sooty silver round the dead girl's neck. Falcon did that.

'It's the one Thomasin had,' he said. 'They exchanged necklaces. It's her.'

The men were watching, so Jankin did not kneel to touch Anna's body, or speak to her. But he took off his jerkin and spread it over her.

'She would have been a great lady,' he said. 'We would have ruled this place well. Our sons and daughters would have been the pride and the power of all the north. Bury her as near to the church as you can, and with honour.'

This time he did kneel, to place a finger against her neck, just in case – but of course she was dead. The light was out. He went down the stairs again to the Great Hall and sat down in Sir Hugh's chair, aware of the gaping space beside him. He had dreamed of this day, of taking his place in the Great Hall with Anna on his arm, placing her with honour in the chair beside him. Whatever anyone thought of him he would have won the greatest trophy in the north of England, and all the fine lords and knights who wanted her would have had to settle for spoilt ugly girls with fortunes.

He was lord of wreck and destruction, of a burned castle and a dead lady. Anna had been a flicker of beauty and gentleness. He turned to look at the empty chair as if a miracle had to happen, and she would be there. It was as if he had loved her.

Had he? He didn't know. He had never loved anyone. He tramped through his castle, hearing its rooms echo. Pushing open a door he found a wide curtained bed, not slept in, and an empty chest that might once have held Anna's clothes. There was nobody to see, so he pressed his face against the sheet where she might have rested.

That body might not be Anna. Setting the power of his own will against death and chaos, he leapt up the stairs, finding the body still there with his jerkin over it. He wrenched the jerkin away, and wisps of sooty thread flew around him.

It was her height – he could tell that from what was left. Her figure, too, but the same could go for any lass in the castle. Her hands were too burned to show if she had done servant's work or not. Her face…

Oh, God. The place where her face should be.

The necklace told him it was Anna.

The dagger told him it was Anna.

Gently, he replaced the jerkin. He wanted to tell her he was sorry, but did not know how.

Warmth suddenly touched his back, and, turning, he was dazzled. She had come back!

She had not. It was only a shaft of sunlight falling through the broken window. For the first time since his childhood, pain and frustration overwhelmed him, and with a howl he drew his sword and crashed it on to the fallen beam. Soot and rags blew up. A body collapsed in on itself.

Falcon and a man called Langstaff, coming to collect the body, heard the cry and the blow. A crow, pecking at bodies, took to its wings and flapped into the sky. Langstaff twisted his mouth.

'Bit late for him to be feeling like that,' he said.

'Hold your tongue,' said Falcon. Langstaff looked at him sideways.

'She was just a lassie,' he muttered. 'A lovely lass.'

'And you're Hawk Jankin's man, and don't forget it,' said Falcon, but as if his mind were somewhere else. Then he held out his arm to keep Langstaff back.

Hawk Jankin was coming towards them. A small bundle,

wrapped in a sheet, lay across his arms. A slender, blistered foot swung from it.

'Off with your cap, Langstaff,' ordered Falcon quietly.

When Thomasin found her voice, she screamed. She screeched out curses, she hammered on the door until her fists were swollen and bleeding, she threw fragments of fragments. She screamed Anna's name, finding that nothing else could blot out the pain where Anna had been, and went on screaming it until her lungs hurt and her throat rasped and burned. She kicked ashes from the grate and screamed for her dagger, because she thought that if she cut herself she could let out the pain. Nobody brought her dagger, so she cut herself on broken pottery and window glass leaving jagged rents in her arms, but the pain did not go away. She rattled the door, threw herself on the floor, took off her shoes and pounded the floor, the fireplace and the walls.

Three of them came to bring her bread and ale, two to hold her while one put the trencher on the table, but as soon as she was free she flung it at the wall. Picking up the cup she realized that she was thirsty, so she gulped mouthfuls of ale before hurling the cup at the door. The drink made her able to scream again, and she screamed, cried and sobbed herself into an exhausted sleep.

Flames roared up in her dreams. Anna was smiling at her, sitting down on the chest, handing her the hairbrush as if nothing had happened. Thomasin woke to the damp night cold, the hard floor and a burning throat. One side of her face ached where Jankin had hit her; she was scratched and bruised, her arms were cut, and the torn, aching place in her heart was unendurable.

If only we had stayed here. I was here to look after her. I promised Lady Isabel.

She didn't know how many days and nights it was. She drifted into nightmares and woke up shaking. She dreamed of Anna, alive and smiling, and woke up broken and raging with disappointment. She ate nothing, drank only enough to ease her raw throat, and yelled curses at Jankin and Falcon, not caring whether they heard her. She still struggled when the men came to bring her food and drink, but not so hard. The will to fight was weakening, but hate remained.

She still had poison. She could finish it all with a mouthful of poison, but she was keeping that for Jankin.

On the other side of the door, Jankin and Falcon drank wine in Jankin's chamber.

'Can you still hear her?' asked Jankin.

'She's stopped,' said Falcon.

Jankin held up his hand for silence. 'I can still hear her,' he said. 'Just have her, Falcon. That'll keep her quiet.'

Falcon shrugged. 'She'd give birth to a dragon,' he said.

Hawk gave a snort of laughter and looked down into his tankard. 'Is it bad luck to force a virgin, Falcon? Is it bad luck to kill one?'

Falcon didn't argue. Hawk had never worried about such things before, but he talked strangely now. He slept badly too, crying out in the night, and waking up sweating. Even when they assured him that Thomasin had stopped screaming, Jankin said he could still hear her. At every corner there were shadows which caused him to whisk round with his dagger in his hand.

Why shouldn't the shades of Hollylaw come to reproach him? In his nightmares Anna floated towards him, smiling sweetly, but how could she smile with no face? He would walk to the bed where his young wife lay, draw back the sheet and find a burned corpse with no face. He slept with his drawn sword in his hand, and woke with a cry when it clattered from his grip. Anyone who approached him quietly and startled him was met with an outburst of fury and the flat of his sword. He drank excessively. On the third night, he asked Falcon again, 'Has she stopped?'

'She's stopped,' said Falcon.

'I can still hear her.' He listened hard, and sprang up. 'Is she dead, then?'

'No, not dead.'

Jankin sprang up. 'How do you know? Go and look, man!'

Wearily, Falcon stood up.

Thomasin could no longer scream. She couldn't understand why she had screamed at all, like a spoilt child kicking on the floor. A strong woman would not behave like that, and she must be strong, even though now there was no Anna to be strong for.

She cried a little, quietly, when she remembered that she was young, an orphan, and the nearest thing she had had to a mother had been killed and could not help her. But it was no good thinking like that. Nobody would offer her pity, so she curled up and rocked herself to and fro. She was rocking Thomasin the motherless child, hushing her and putting her to bed. Then she dried her eyes, took a few deep breaths and picked up her spindle. She still had that, and Anna's spindle, too. She hadn't the heart to spin now, but she pressed the friendly shape to her heart, where poison still lay. When the door opened she stood up, painfully, to face it.

Falcon. It was often Falcon, but beyond him she could see the flare of red hair, the skinny red beard, and that face – without a sound she raised the spindle and lurched forward. There was horror in Jankin's eyes. Falcon caught her, and turned, jamming her back against himself, forcing her hand until her fingers opened and the precious spindle dropped to the floor. She struggled and made a feeble kick, but she had little strength left to fight now. Before the door banged shut again, she had crumpled on the floor. Falcon had taken her spindle, and she hated him more bitterly than ever.

There was still Anna's, but she was too drained to reach for it. She hugged her knees, closed her eyes, and rocked silently.

In his chamber, Jankin was shaking. It was as if the fury that had filled and sent him raging and burning through Hollylaw had settled in Thomasin's eyes. Her anger was his anger.

'What's that?' he demanded. 'A knife?'

Falcon dropped it on to the floor. 'A woman's spindle,' he said, and stood looking at it. Such a thing had not been seen for a long time in this fortress of men. He was glad he had been able to force it from her so easily. He would not have liked to bang her knuckles on the stones, or stamp on her fingers.

Whispers ran round the tower like vermin. What was Jankin playing at? He didn't have to take the castle that night. Why didn't he just turn round and bring us all back?

'Why do we follow him?'

'He's jumpy. He's overreaching himself now. Doesn't know where he's going. Is he going to kill the other one?'

'He can't let her live.'

'She's just a lass. It's a shame. One's enough. Unlucky enough.'

'And she has spirit. Shame to kill her.'

'And he's already killed the best of them. No bringing back the Flower of Hollylaw. The lass came up here looking like an angel.'

'But seeing as he's killed one, he may as well kill the other. What does she have to live for now? She's off her head, or she soon will be.'

'She's a hellcat.'

'Unlucky to kill one like that.'

'Can't let her live.'

'What does Falcon think?'

'Who ever knows what Falcon thinks?'

How many days? Five, and five nights. Thomasin had lost count. So had Jankin. Falcon knew.

'The shadow maid has to die,' said Jankin. 'Her curses are coming upon me already. They'll stop if she's dead.' He scowled, turning his empty cup round in his hands. 'Will it stop, or not? It'll be worse. It will be worse if I kill her. No blood. Shedding her blood would be unlucky.'

Falcon refilled his cup. 'I'll do it,' he said calmly. 'You gave her to me, and I've had my fill of her tears and tantrums. I'll put her down the Linn.'

Chapter Seven

In a broad green valley about fifteen miles from Hollylaw stood Hallowburn Abbey, the home of the Grey Sisters of the Magnificat. The abbey itself was small and simply built of pale stone, with fishponds and orchards, cowsheds and chickens, and spreading, well-tended gardens. The sisters were dedicated to worship and prayer. They met together to sing praises to God at the set hours, and prayed alone in their cells. But they were also a healing order, and the old, injured and infirm were often brought to their care. In these lawless lands they were used to receiving the survivors of battles. These smooth skinned women, with their white wimples and plain grey habits, their sweet voices and holy lives, had treated huge bleeding gashes, twisted limbs, and weeping and festering flesh that would turn the stomach of a strong man. When the first stragglers from Hollylaw hobbled into sight, struggling to carry those too badly injured to walk, the nuns already had bandages and cooling lotions prepared.

Mother Gabriel, the abbess, saw them first, when they were still shuffling down the hill and through the meadow where the cows grazed. The news of the sack of Hollylaw had not yet reached her but at once she called for clean towels, sheets and hot water, and sent young novices running from the gatehouse to receive the visitors. With scorched rags of clothes, grubbily dressed injuries, and dirty tear-stained faces, all who were left from Hollylaw limped into the nunnery. The children whimpered quietly and dragged their feet. The dying were carried on hurdles.

'We need infusions of St John's wort,' ordered Mother Gabriel, 'and yarrow, lady's mantle, chamomile, marigold. And Sister Agnes's mixture to soothe pain – tell her that we need her to make more. Sisters, bring in fresh comfrey to make poultices.' She stretched out her hands to the exhausted travellers. 'Welcome, in the name of Jesus Christ and Our Lady of the Magnificat.'

When wounds had been washed and soothed and cool drinks given, Mother Gabriel asked questions. What had happened? Where was Lady Isabel? Nobody knew. Some had seen her running to the stairs with a sword in her hands. What had happened to the daughter? Had she been there? Oh, yes. Somebody had seen her going back into the castle, for there were still children in there. Somebody else remembered seeing her on the stairs – she and some of the serving girls had been trying to protect the children.

'Mother Abbess, she talked to me. She showed us where the moat was easiest to cross, where there were woods on the other side. We got boards from the cellar to float on. She told us to go quickly. She had the little ones in her arms; she ran with them. We had to do as she said.'

The most seriously ill were kept apart from the others. Some had caught infections from swimming the moat. The sisters watched them, and a priest was sent for. Mother Gabriel gently lifted away the damp and sooty blankets, and sighed. Most would not survive the night, and it might be better that way.

From a mattress on the floor came a low sound, a subdued gasp of pain so young, so childlike in its need, that Mother

Gabriel's heart hurt. She knelt by the mattress, and, seeing a hand that was not burned, touched it gently.

'Peace, child,' she said, and turned to the sisters. 'Put this one in a cell by herself. Move her very gently. I will look after this child myself. Send for a priest, because many of them will die in the night. This one... she should have the last rites of the church.'

Waves of pain washed through Anna, another and another, and when she could no longer fight she gave in to them. With each surge of pain she tried to tell herself that this would be the last, but it never was. When she drifted into sleep, nightmares of fire claimed her. When she woke, she still saw fire. She tried to call for her mother, but knew that her mother would not hear her.

Her memories were blurred, but pictures stayed with her. Thomasin. She remembered Thomasin's face as the dice tumbled from her fingers. Where were they now? Anna must have reached Hollylaw – she remembered telling her mother something – and Thomasin was... where was Thomasin?

The pain struck like claws through her arm, her side, her shoulder, her ear, her face. It sank white hot teeth into the space behind her eyes. It stung her lips.

Someone slipped water into her mouth. Cool and sweet, it rippled across the cracked lips and over her hugely swollen tongue. From sleep she drifted into a long, dull, throbbing ache and sudden spears of hot pain if she moved. How long had it lasted? Years? The voices around her changed. There were kind voices, cold, bitter drinks in her mouth and salves on her skin. She lay still and, at last, slept deeply and woke with her head clear.

There was still pain, but it was bearable. A cool damp cloth covered half her face and neck. All the left side of her body seemed to be covered with dressings that eased the sting of pain. An arch the colour of sand was above her, and the air felt clean. Voices whispered nearby, and a skirt swished. Cautiously she turned her head, but the movement hurt so much that she cried out without meaning to. Sandalled feet stepped near to her.

'Shh,' said a voice. 'Be still.' It was the voice of a woman, as fine and cultivated as her mother's, but softer, and soothing. 'You've wakened properly. God be thanked.'

Anna tried to turn towards the speaker, but again, the movement hurt. A blurred face appeared above her, a kind, wimpled face, with the wrinkles of age but the freshness of a girl. 'I'll try not to hurt you,' said the nun.

Anna tried to bite her lip, but even that movement was painful. The nun very gently lifted the cooling pad from her face and bent to look. Sudden light made her blink and frown.

'Does the light give you pain?' asked the nun. She looked closely at the left side of Anna's face and laid the cloth lightly back in place with a note of approval in her voice. 'That's healing.'

Anna tried to ask what happened, but her voice could only manage a few blurred sounds. It was as if she had forgotten how to speak, and had to make the words out of nothing.

'What happened?' she whispered.

'You were badly burned, and they brought you here,' said the nun. 'You're safe now.' With a horn teaspoon, she poured drops of water into Anna's mouth. 'I'm Mother Gabriel. Can you tell me your name?'

Anna nearly told her, but did not. Who was she now? She was Jankin's lawful wife. If anyone knew who she was she might have to go back to him, and she couldn't face that now.

She tried to ask what had happened at Hollylaw, but it was too difficult.

She slept again, woke in pain, and cried out. Mother Gabriel hurried in, with a young sister behind her carrying a bowl and towels. The nun changed Anna's dressings while Anna gripped Mother Gabriel's hands and groaned through her teeth when she couldn't help it. Once, she found she was saying something about her mother.

'I don't know, child,' said Mother Gabriel gently. When Anna fell asleep again, Mother Gabriel sat in the lamplight, watching her.

Most of the survivors from Hollylaw had now left the abbey to take refuge with family elsewhere. Of those who remained, nobody seemed to know who this girl was. Most of her clothing had been burned away, but what remained was intriguing. Who would wear a bodice like that, embroidered with beads? And why the silver? Mother Gabriel rinsed and rubbed the beads, and looked again. Round, innocent pearls gleamed milkily back at her.

As to identifying her by what she looked like – that wasn't worth considering, poor love. But the hand Mother Gabriel held – the undamaged right hand – was not the hand of a peasant. She herself had washed this hand and found a soft palm with smooth, pale fingers.

It was well known by now that Lady Isabel and the Flower of Hollylaw were dead and buried, and the maid was said to be a prisoner at High Crag Tower. So who was this?

The girl stirred and muttered in her sleep. She said something, but words blurred and slurred so that Mother Gabriel had to lean close to listen. Something about sins?

'Ma sin,' whispered the girl, and said it again, her voice growing high. 'Ma... sin!'

Mother Gabriel stroked her right hand. 'All your sins are forgiven, my dear,' she said. 'We sent for a priest. He gave you absolution.'

'Om… ma… sin.'

'You are free from all your sins,' said Mother Gabriel. 'You can make confession to the priest when you are well enough, if that comforts you. Now, sleep.'

A tear slipped down Anna's face. It stung and burned.

In the following days, Anna was less asleep and more awake. The pain became less severe and less frequent. Speaking, coughing, yawning and swallowing still hurt. The sight in her left eye was poor and most of that side of her body was scarred, blotched and too sore to touch. Even as it healed the skin remained rough and discoloured. Once she put her fingers to her face and, not liking what she felt, decided not to do that again. Each day there was a little less pain and a little more movement, though her voice was thick and her lips seemed not to belong to her. Taking her weight on her feet was painful, but she could walk a few steps.

They had given her a white shift to wear, which was softer than the coarse fabric worn by the nuns and would not irritate her skin, and a nun's cell had been set apart for her with a window to the garden. Voices reached her. She could see leaves drifting on the grass, nuns and lay women carrying baskets of apples and pears, and the daily changing sky. When garden fires were lit and the waft of woodsmoke left her crying, screaming, pouring with sweat and shaking, Mother Gabriel sent sisters to comfort and hold her, and hang a screen in front of the window so that she would not have to experience again the smell of burning. The sweet, sharp aroma of fruit cooking wafted through to her, and

Mother Gabriel would bring her little dishes of baked apples and honey. When anyone asked her name she did not answer, and Mother Gabriel chose not to press the question. 'Child' or 'sister' was all anyone called her. That would do. Gradually Anna noticed that the Hollylaw voices had all gone away, and the voices of the sisters became familiar to her.

Her memories of what had happened in Hollylaw were still patchy and confusing. There were some things she dared not ask Mother Gabriel. Now that the pain was not so terrible, she was glad of Mother Gabriel's visits and welcomed the fragrance of the infusions and the sight of the earthenware bowl and clean towels. She could even bring herself to watch as Mother Gabriel lifted back her sleeve and examined the blotched, healing skin.

Anna spoke with difficulty. Her mouth still hurt, and would not open properly on one side, thickening her speech.

'They're all gone,' she said.

'Gone? Oh, the people from Hollylaw,' said Mother Gabriel. 'You have good healing skin, I think. They have gone to their relatives, or back to Hollylaw.'

'But…' the name was too difficult to say. 'That man!'

Mother Gabriel glanced up from the dressing. 'Jankin the Hawk?' she said. 'He does not seem to be troubling Hollylaw just now. I suppose he has what he wanted. Do you think you could walk a few steps this morning? As far as the window?'

By slow stages, day by day, Anna found she could walk without holding on to anyone or anything. She could get to the window by herself, and lean on the sill. Late on an autumn day she looked out to the gold and deep red of the quiet garden. It was a chilly afternoon, with bruised apples and shabby fallen leaves lying in clusters about the tree roots. A young nun, a novice, was crossing the grass with firewood in her arms. Her sandalled feet and the hem of her habit were damp, and the veil and wimple surrounded her face so neatly that she seemed to be looking out through a frame. *Like a nun in a portrait frame*, thought Anna.

Anna's own frame was the window. She observed the nun as if they stood in different worlds, each in her own picture frame. The nun continued her walk, bending to pick up a dropped branch, as if Anna were invisible.

But Anna was not invisible. The nun drew nearer, looked down to shake her wet hem from her ankles and, as she straightened up, looked directly at Anna. Anna tried to smile at her, but pain and disfigurement made it a grimace.

The nun shrieked. The firewood fell from her arms and her hands flew to her mouth. Above those hands, there was such horror in her eyes that she might have seen a demon. She bent hurriedly, scrabbled her armful of firewood clumsily together and ran.

Anna sank down on the window seat, suddenly feeling sick. Tears and the straining of her face burned into her.

Night fell. The singing of the nuns in the chapel ceased, and they glided back to their cells in silence. Mother Gabriel brought her candles. Now she came to think of it, it was always Mother Gabriel and the older, senior nuns who attended to her needs. No young and sensitive sister was allowed near.

The sky was clear that night. With an effort that made her grit her teeth, Anna struggled to the window and leaned forward to peer into the glass.

A hideous mask looked sullenly back at her. It was made of lumps of discoloured skin, livid scars, one half closed eye, a lopsided mouth and a few remaining tufts of hair sprouting through a blotched scalp.

She hobbled back to bed. Once, in a story, there had been a beautiful girl called Anna. She was so lovely that everyone called her the Flower of Hollylaw, and everybody she met loved her. She could sing and dance, and had good friends and beautiful clothes, and lived in a castle. But it had only been a story.

The next day, when the nuns went to sing their midday psalms, Anna stood in the shadow of the abbey church doorway. When Mother Gabriel came to the cell to dress her burns, she asked if she might have a veil to wear over her face.

'It isn't for vanity, Mother Abbess,' she said. 'I don't want to distress the sisters.'

Mother Gabriel sat on the window seat and folded her large, strong hands.

'How did you know what you looked like?' she asked.

'I looked at my reflection,' she answered.

'And?'

Anna gave a shrug that was not as careless as it was meant to look. 'I'm still alive,' she said. 'It's only a face. But,' she almost smiled, 'I'm not the one who has to look at it, so I would like a veil.'

'And a name?' said Mother Gabriel. She did not let her eyes stray to the smooth young hand, but she was intensely aware of it, as if that hand tried to speak to her and tell her its past. When Anna did not answer, she went on, 'When you were ill, you cried out about your sins, and we sent for the priest to give you absolution.'

Anna's fingertips tingled. 'What did I say?' she gasped.

'Nothing to trouble yourself with,' said Mother Gabriel

gently. 'You were saying, "My sin! All my sin!" We assumed that you meant you wanted to be forgiven.' Her eyes were not unkind, but there was a steadiness about them that held Anna's gaze. 'Perhaps, child, you have forgotten who you are.'

Anna looked away and took a deep breath before she found her voice. Before saying anything about who she was, she needed to know the truth.

'Please tell me,' she said. 'I'm strong enough to hear it now. What happened at Hollylaw?'

Gravely, steadily, Mother Gabriel told her all she knew. She told her the tales she had learned from the fleeing peasants and servants, with their news of the few who had survived and the many who had not. When Mother Gabriel told her that Lady Isabel was dead, Anna looked down and bit her lip, because she might give herself away if she wept for her mother.

'I'm sorry to have to tell you such news, child,' said Mother Gabriel.

Anna's face tingled with heat, and she wondered if her skin still showed blushes. 'What about Anna,' she asked steadily, 'the one they called the Flower?'

'Anna Lillie,' said Mother Gabriel. The sound of her own name shivered through Anna. The abbess's eyes were blue-grey and as sharp as sword points.

'Anna's body was found in the castle, near to her mother's,' she said. 'She was badly burned. They identified her by a necklace she wore, and buried her with honour. Is the light in your eyes?'

Anna frowned as she tried to remember. Necklace? Had she been wearing one? She tried to visualize necklaces. Thomasin would know. She always did.

'There was a maidservant,' she said. 'Her name was Tho...' She could not go on.

That evening, while Anna slept, two travellers called for shelter at the abbey. They slept in the guest house and left at dawn, but by then Mother Gabriel had coaxed their story from them. In her cold cell she knelt before a candle and a crucifix, thinking and praying. The visitors had not said that they were Jankin's men running away, and there was no point in asking them, but she was quite sure. How much of their story could she tell to the girl from Hollylaw? That was all she could call her. The girl from Hollylaw. If the ladies of the family and Anna's maid were dead, what gentlewoman was this?

According to the visitors, Hawk Jankin was losing his wits, seeing terrifying visions by day and night, suddenly flaring into rages, crashing the door behind him and locking himself in, not always hearing what was said to him, sleeping with his drawn sword in his hand. Unable to sleep, he would rise early to ride the moors. Sometimes he returned muttering about ghosts in the mists reaching out to him, the vengeful ghost of Lady Isabel, the tearful ghosts of the children of Hollylaw, the beautiful, sorrowful ghost of his bride as the flames destroyed her – and the other one.

The band of outlaws at High Crag Tower were turning to Falcon to lead them, or leaving altogether. What Jankin had done at Hollylaw had been too much, even for them. He had killed the Flower of Hollylaw.

In the morning Mother Gabriel saw the girl from Hollylaw, veiled, limping into the chapel for prayers. When the nuns had returned to their cells and their work, she laid a gentle hand on Anna's fingers.

'Sit down, child,' she said. It was hard to tell this, but it must be done, and Mother Gabriel did it as clearly and as gently as she could.

'There was a maidservant,' she said gently. 'Her name was Thomasin.'

'Yes?' gasped Anna.

'I am so sorry,' said Mother Gabriel. 'I'm told she died. One of Jankin's men killed her.'

Anna lowered her head into her hands and wished she, too, could die. She wanted to die now, without ever having to look up again. Mother Gabriel put a hand on the shoulder which did not hurt.

'I'm so sorry,' she said. 'I'm so sorry, Anna.' It was a guess, but a considered one.

Anna turned her head and lifted back the veil. One eye could only half open. The other was red with sorrow.

'Please don't tell anyone,' she said. 'Please, Mother Gabriel. They're all gone except me. I can't be who I was without them. I never want to be Anna again.'

Chapter Eight

Falcon slept badly, and woke to a grim morning. Jankin had always been part of Falcon's life, as much as his own blood and bone. It had been so since they were part of a pack of small boys, and Jankin, the leader and the hero, had let his younger cousin join in. As they grew, he had given Falcon the place at his right hand and a training in how to ride, fight, hunt and survive in the wild borderlands. Falcon had become his brother in arms, his bodyguard, and the first to share danger and glory. They had saved each other's lives, and killed for each other. Jankin's authority had a voice in Falcon. Their weapons and women had always been their own, but they shared all other things. Their lives were woven together.

Years of hard riding, hard fighting and hard living had taught Falcon more than how to be Jankin's right hand. It had taught him Jankin's law. He had warned Jankin of Thomasin, and Jankin had openly scorned him. That was not how things should be done. If Falcon allowed himself to be treated like a minion, he would become one. He would lose respect. For the first time, he questioned his loyalty.

He hadn't spent half an hour in Thomasin's company before he knew she was not to be trusted. She had a prim little face, always at her mistress's side, watching, gliding quietly about in her grey gown as if she wanted to be invisible. There was something cat-like about Thomasin, a creature who would watch and watch until she sprang with her claws outstretched. He was certain she had tried to poison Jankin at the wedding and that the escape on the wedding night had not been Anna's idea. And now the grey shadow lay curled in her chamber among the remnants of a broken chair and shards of smashed pottery, cursing him and lapsing into silence. She had grown as thin and haggard as a winter starveling, her hair wild, her eyes pink with grief and sleeplessness, staring with hate. The men said she was a witch, bringing down curses on them all. He had told the dungheads guarding her to bring clean spring water and wine to wash the cuts on her arms, and they had done it grudgingly.

What if she really were a witch? Falcon sat up and swore quietly. She was too much for him, whatever else she might be.

Jankin had not been himself since the burning of Hollylaw. He thought Anna was haunting him, but now he wanted this one dead too. Another one to haunt him? This was the day when Falcon must throw her down the Linn, and his heart twisted away from the thought of it.

He stood up, stretched out the stiffness from his limbs, and pulled his jerkin over his shirt. There was still his horse to be saddled, and food and water to be put in a satchel before he marched up the spiral staircase where Clem and Nick guarded the door.

'She'll give you no trouble, sir,' said Clem, but Falcon, striding past them, felt the glance they exchanged behind his back. In the next second Clem found himself pinned against the wall with Falcon's fist pressed into his throat.

'Sorry…' he wheezed, '… sir.'

'For what?' demanded Falcon.

'For disrespect, sir,' Clem gasped, his eyes watering. 'I only meant –' Falcon loosened his grip just enough to let him say exactly what he meant '– that she's a demon.' Falcon held him until his eyes bulged before releasing him and holding out a hand for the keys.

Thomasin sat on the floor, propped up against the wall, her legs stretched in front of her like a rag doll, pale and straggle-haired. Her arms looked as if a beast had savaged her. There was no expression in her eyes as she looked up at Falcon.

'She's had enough, sir,' said Nick.

'I'll have her tied, all the same,' said Falcon. 'I know what those nails can do. Gently! Look at the state of her arms!' He could afford to say that now, having reminded them who he was. She did not struggle as they roped her hands together, then her ankles.

Thomasin stared blankly in front of her. *Is it nearly over now?*

Everything she loved and lived for in the world had gone. Her home, Anna, Lady Isabel, all the friends she ever had, all gone for ever, and it was all her fault. She had spied on Jankin, she had helped Anna to get out, and now everything lay in ashes. Whole families were dead, and it was her fault. Her knives had been taken away from her, and even her spindle. Perhaps it was no longer having the spindle hanging at her waist that finally broke her. All she had left was a small bottle of poison and the will to use it if she did not die instantly at High Crag Linn. Maybe Falcon would run her through with his sword first. He was hauling her to her feet.

'Sir,' said Nick, and for a moment he laid a large, rough hand on Falcon's sleeve, 'she's only a lass.'

'I know that,' said Falcon gruffly, and realized that his arm was around Thomasin's shoulders as if he were her brother or lover, not her executioner. 'Where's her cloak?'

Clem might have thought that she wouldn't need it for long, but he kept his thoughts to himself. Falcon threw the cloak – Anna's cloak – around Thomasin and stooped to lift her in his arms and carry her to the horse that stamped and snorted in the morning mist. Clem took her as Falcon swung into the saddle, and was about to throw her across the pommel.

'She can sit up, can't she?' growled Falcon. Clem looked as if he would have argued that she couldn't sit sideways on a cross saddle, but he'd already angered Falcon once. He hoisted Thomasin sideways to the front of the saddle.

'Do you want her tying on, sir?'

Falcon ignored him, clamping one arm round Thomasin's waist and taking the reins in the other. Then he looked down at Clem, standing by the stirrup.

'Only a lassie,' he said, with no expression on his face, and Clem smiled as he slapped the horse's rump. The harness jangled.

Thomasin pushed her tied hands against the front of the saddle and, because she had a little pride left, forced herself to sit upright. Her fingers curled on the worn leather and she clutched it as she clutched the hope that she would be dead the very second she struck the rocks beneath the waterfall, and that she would meet Anna again. Heaven would smell of lavender and be filled with music sweeter than the music of minstrels, sweeter than the music she and Anna used to sing together, sweeter than Christmas music, even sweeter than the singing boys in the huge church in town. All would be clean and fresh, and it would be springtime.

She thought of the hermit who lived in caves at the bottom of High Crag Linn. He had been known to rescue Jankin's victims and nurse them, but Thomasin did not know if she wanted to be rescued. The horse clopped steadily uphill. Falcon was silent, his arm tight about her waist. She shivered. It was a damp morning, and beginning to drizzle. She was hungry.

Falcon let the reins fall on the horse's neck and wrapped Thomasin's cloak more tightly round her. Old habits made her feel she should thank him, but she did not. He held it in place around her waist as he rode on, looking ahead.

Her face was turned away from him, and all he could see of her were the dark curls and a swathe of cloak. He found he was wondering what would have happened if he had grown up learning to love honour, chivalry and gentleness. For the first time in his life, he dreamed of a different Falcon. Perhaps there could have been a Falcon who had led a clean life and could ask Lady Isabel's permission to marry her daughter's handmaid, and he wondered, if that could have happened, whether Thomasin would have had him. Looking down, it was all he could do not to kiss the tangled hair.

Pressed against Falcon, Thomasin found she was glad of his warmth. It would have been warmer still, and even comforting, to relax her huddled shoulders and lean her head back against his shoulder. But she wasn't so demeaned as to do that, not when he was taking her to kill her and she still intended to spit in his face first.

The mists were clearing, and she tried to take an interest in the waking world. There was birdsong, dew and a clear sky, pleasant in the way that a well-finished piece of wool or weaving was pleasant, but nothing to stay alive for. She closed her eyes, recited a prayer in her head and tried to bring Anna's face to the dark space behind her eyes. When she looked again she was higher on the moors than she had ever been in her life, and could hear something; what was it? Rushing wind? Thunder? Whatever it was, it was louder every minute until she could hear that it was more than one sound; there was shouting and roaring, gush, splash. Not far away she could see a cloud that was not a cloud, but a fine spray...

Oh God, have mercy. She had never thought a waterfall could be so terrifying. Her fingers tightened. In her heart she soothed herself as she would have soothed Anna: *courage, my love, courage. It will all be over soon. Is there an angel for me?*

If ever a land needed angels, it was this one. Maybe there were angels for England and angels for Scotland, but no angels for this borderland, only an angel of death that stood to one side with folded hands and folded wings to watch as she fell down High Crag Linn and lean over the edge to see her break on the rocks.

Falcon pulled on the reins as she had known he would. A burning of fear ran through her. She hadn't thought she cared if she lived or died, but now, on the edge of a waterfall, life was all she had, and it was precious. It was terrible to lose it here, bedraggled, dirty and hungry, with nobody who cared about her. When Falcon swung down from the horse, she tried to dismount by herself but he dragged her down from the saddle, still holding her before him. With her tied feet she could not kick, but she stamped down hard on his feet. Her thin shoes had no effect on his tall leather boots, but she would fight. Over the roaring of the waterfall he was shouting something, but she was determined not to hear him.

'Listen to me, Thomasin,' he yelled. She tried to kick, but he kicked back so that her legs buckled and he forced her to her knees with her wrists in one hand.

'Do you want to give yourself a chance?' he yelled over the waterfall. 'Be still, and listen! Listen to me!'

'Burn in deepest hell!' snarled Thomasin.

'Aye, I will,' he said. 'But not yet. Stop fighting, I'm not going to hurt you.' She almost laughed, and his grip tightened. 'We may both be lost, Thomasin, but not if I can help it. Come to the edge. Do as I say, or I can't help you.'

She tried to shout that she didn't want his help, but he could not or would not hear her. When he shouted that she must trust him she would have laughed, but she couldn't laugh any more. If he wanted to help her, why had he dragged her to the edge of the falls?

She tried to remember what she should pray. *Lord have mercy, Christ have mercy, Lord have mercy, Ave Maria, gratia plena...* A sob escaped her and she hated herself for shame. Help her? Falcon, help her?

He was holding her at the cliff edge. Beyond her toes water hurtled over stones, further and further down, strong and wild to the rocks, the dizzying fall. *Oh God, have mercy...*

He pinioned her arms. Water and fear pounded in her ears.

'Press your feet down hard!' he yelled, and pushed her down as if he would plant her into the ground. Then he had picked her up and was carrying her back to the horse, throwing her into the saddle, leaping up behind her, urging the horse to a canter, and High Crag Linn was behind them with its hungry roar fading, and a wild moorland of heather, birch and broom was ahead.

In the days and nights at High Crag Tower she had learned not to ask questions. She might not be told the truth, and if she were, she might not like to know it. But she could listen for the rasp of weapons in case Falcon drew his sword. She was weak from imprisonment and the days when she could eat nothing. Thirst made her throat burn. She struggled to sit upright in the saddle. When Falcon guided the horse into a copse of birch trees, her heart sickened. *Why bring me here? Why couldn't he have just killed me at the Linn?* Slowly, confidently, at Falcon's guiding, the horse came to a clearing a little way downhill, where Falcon reined it in.

'Don't be afraid,' he said. He lifted her down and held on to her as if she would crumple and fall if he let go – as she might, he thought. She must be dizzy and bruised. 'Sit down.'

He let go and she sank to the ground with her eyes on the knife at his waist, but it was not his knife he reached for. From the satchel at his shoulder he opened a leather bottle, and offered it to her. Though her wrists were bound, her hands were free enough to hold it. If she had trusted him, she would have grabbed at it.

'Look,' he said, 'it's safe.' He drank from the bottle. She found she was watching intently as he gulped down water, hoping there would be some left. When he held it out to her again, water glistening on his hand and mouth, she drank.

From the satchel he took rough bread, broke it, and handed her a piece. It was dry and stale, but it was bread, and she felt stronger for eating it. When he knelt in front of her and reached for his knife she squirmed away, but with two swift cuts he slashed through the cords binding her hands and feet. He then took her hands in his and turned them, pouring water on the cuts, asking her if the cords had hurt her.

Thomasin flexed her fingers, wrists and arms, and forgot, for the moment, to spit in his face, but she strained away from him. Falcon had not thrown her down the Linn and now he was treating her kindly, but he was still Falcon. She clenched her hands and bit her lip. Whatever he planned, she could still fight with her nails and teeth. She could beg for mercy, but she wouldn't. She looked directly into his eyes.

'I had to take you to the edge,' he said. For the first time she saw earnestness in his eyes and heard it in his voice. He was speaking gently to her, and nobody had been gentle since Anna left. 'If Jankin goes to High Crag Linn to see the evidence for himself, he'll see your footprints at the edge, and only mine coming back. Now, you must go.'

She tried to speak, and could not. He let go of her wrists, and held her shoulders still.

'Listen to me, Thomasin. Do exactly as I say. There is a track that leads between that hill, the flat-topped hill – look at it, Thomasin, you can't see it if you don't turn round and look! Between that hill and the crag to the right of it. You'll go downhill, then over the river and up the other side of the valley. When you get over the hills there's a farmstead or two and then you come down to a market town. Are you taking this in? There are stepping stones over the river. Two days' journey – three for you, maybe.' He hung the leather strap of the satchel over her shoulder. 'You'll need bread and water. When it gets dark or foggy, take cover, find shelter – don't try to go on. You'd only get lost. Do you understand all this? Say something!'

Her eyes were filling and her voice could not be trusted. She could not even understand why she wanted to cry: because Falcon was being kind, because she was saved or because she had thought it would soon all be over, and now she had to go on? There was to be no death on the stones. There would be more struggle, more pain, more mornings to wake up to. But some might be worth waking up for.

She managed a whisper.

'Why?'

Falcon looked away without answering. She drew away from him, and he did not try to stop her. When a fly settled on her arm he brushed it away, and the sudden movement made her flinch.

'You shouldn't be alone,' muttered Falcon, and Thomasin wasn't sure if he was speaking to her, or to himself. 'I should come with you. I wish I could. But if I didn't come back, Jankin wouldn't rest until he found me, and he mustn't find you, so I have to leave you to go alone. Do you understand?'

Slowly, frowning, she nodded. She saw the concern in his eyes, as if he wasn't sure she could manage this alone. She was so drained and confused, she must look and sound like a simpleton. Somewhere inside her, the true Thomasin must remain with her fighting spirit.

'Why?' she asked again. Her voice was firmer this time.

'You,' he said. 'You, Thomasin.' He leapt to his feet, swirled off his cloak, and wrapped it round her shoulders. 'You'll need an extra cloak, it gets cold at nights. And I have to make Jankin believe that I killed you, so I take a trophy back. It's the way it's always done. I'll have to cut your hair.'

Thomasin nodded, seeing the sense in this. Without a word she lifted up her hair in one hand and stood perfectly still while Falcon's dagger rasped once, twice, three times. A few loose curls tickled her neck and fell on to her arms. There was a chilly gap where her hair had been, and she pulled up the collar of his cloak.

He repeated the directions and told her briefly where she might find streams and shelter. Then he pushed the handful of dark curls inside his jerkin, and mounted the horse.

'If ever you say prayers, remember me,' he muttered. 'Go now. Just go.'

She took a few steps away from him. He pulled on the reins to lift his horse's head.

'And, Thomasin,' he said, 'before I leave you, remember

this. Above everything else, *never* come back to High Crag Tower. Do you understand? If Jankin sees you, if any of them see you and tell him, he won't let you live. Never come back.' He turned the horse to go, and shouted the words over his shoulder as if this, of all things, had to stay with her. 'Never come back!'

Crows flew into the air. The rocks rang. Thomasin backed away, turned and stumbled over the moor. Falcon had already urged the horse to a gallop.

This time, he had made his own decision. He had obeyed his own heart, not Jankin's orders, and he had set a true spirit free. She would have more struggles before her; he thought of her spitting in someone else's face, and smiled. Maybe she'd love, and be loved. Just as likely she'd make some man's life hell. But he hoped she'd be happy.

The only good thing he had ever done must be left behind and never spoken of. He rose in the stirrups and urged the horse on faster.

Chapter Nine

Thomasin looked back once, wishing she could follow Falcon like a lost puppy following anyone it recognized, but she could not go back to a burned village and High Crag Tower. She ran, forgetting hunger and wretchedness, fixing her eyes on the flat-topped hill and the crag which never seemed to come nearer. When exhaustion came over her she forced the next step and the next, though her feet were so sore that every step hurt. The sky grew heavy, hot and thundery, making her head throb. She would stop in the shelter of the next rock – no, the next – no, she could manage a little further. Finally, she set her back against a rock, gulped stale water from the bottle and staggered on before she could become too comfortable.

The hot, close air drained her strength, weighing her down towards earth and drowsiness. The sky was a thick grey fleece above her. Her swollen feet ached and stung until she crawled to the next rock and the first drops of rain fell. She wrapped Falcon's cloak tightly about her and huddled against the rock until the storm had passed.

Trying to stand, she gasped and stumbled. Pain stabbed through her feet. She slumped down beside the rock again, ripping at the hem of her smock until she had strips of cloth to bind round her toes and pad her shoes. That was better. She pulled up the cloak to warm the cold gap where her hair had been, and wove her way between puddles and rocks. It grew darker. Darker. Darker. She must not drink too much water, and the throbbing headache took away every urge to eat. She must walk as far as possible tonight, nearer to the place Falcon had told her of. She had not noticed how dark it was until she stumbled into water and staggered back, gasping and cursing the moors.

A ridge of boulders stood between Thomasin and the hill, and looked as if they might provide the best shelter she would find. She settled against them, pressing as close to a rock as she could, curling up tightly in the cloak, her hand closed around Anna's necklace. The scent and prickle of heather was all around her. In the long hours of darkness she shivered, dozed, dreamed of fire and woke at every owl hoot and bark of a fox. Every time she woke, it was still dark.

Sunrise was cold and sullen, barely penetrating the fog that had woven around her in the night. The unfolding of tightly curled limbs hurt and made her grimace and rub furiously at her legs, but the headache had cleared and she ate a little bread and sipped the water. The bottle was much lighter now.

The best thing now was to climb to the top of the rocks where she had sheltered. It would give her the best possible view of her surroundings; or it would if the fog lifted.

Jankin woke on the floor with a wooden cup in his hand and a sour taste in his mouth. He rolled onto his back, cursed at the roof beams and shambled to his feet.

On the floor lay a black, furry shape and, growling curses against rats, he flung the cup at it. A few curls drifted across the floor.

He rubbed his face, recalling a blurred memory of Falcon coming back with a fistful of the shadow witch's hair and putting it into his hand. What did he want with that, now that she was dead? Now, maybe Anna would go, too. He could not drink her out of his nightmares. He had found her rosary beads in the small chamber at the tower and carried them with him as a talisman, even though they didn't seem to protect him.

He still divided his time between High Crag Tower and his castle at Hollylaw. He should move there permanently. Whatever ghosts it had, they couldn't be worse than the ones that haunted him here. The smell of burning bodies would have gone by now.

He mustn't think of that. Waking with a bellyful of last night's ale, he mustn't think of burning bodies and the girl without a face who had once been Anna, and beautiful, and his. He kicked Falcon awake and jumped down through the trapdoor, demanding a horse and a few strong men to go with him. But the ghosts followed him to Hollylaw and left him slurring his words and losing control. He knew that the men saw it. His castle was a place strange to him, still full of the debris of its fall. A slipper that might have been Anna's lay on the floor. A trick of the light on a wall could be the swish of a hem or the waft of a headdress. He could never be sure what came at him through mist or night. Unable to sleep, he rode out at night into darkness.

Thomasin gritted her teeth, cursed her blisters and refused to cry. She had woken early and tried to go on before daylight, but now feared that she might have been going round in circles, or worse, back to High Crag Tower. There was a hill, though she had no idea which, and a sound of water which might be a spring, and the water bottle was empty. By the time she had found the spring, filled the bottle and climbed to a high place, the mist might have cleared and she could work out which way to go next.

She wouldn't eat yet. If she ate the bread now she couldn't have it later. The sun rose a little higher; the mist was not as thick as it had been. She found a slope and began to climb, mist leaving droplets clinging to her hair and clothes. Falcon's cloak encumbered her, so she took it off and left it spread on a rock as she clambered up. At last she stood on a high peak, turning slowly, taking in the landscape in every direction. The pass between the flat-topped hill and the steep crag was clear now, and seemed much nearer than it had last night. She could make good progress before night fell again, though her shoes hurt so much that it would be easier to walk in bare feet.

She could hear something far off, and turned towards the sound, feeling as well as hearing it. It was the beat of a horse's hooves. She shrank down, groping among the rocks until her hand closed on a loose, sharp stone.

The rider was coming closer. It might be somebody who would help, or it could be Falcon, changing his mind, playing cat and mouse with her. Or – she flinched at the thought of his name – it might be Hawk Jankin, knowing she was still alive and hunting her down. The hoof beats came nearer, and she shivered. It was as if some shadowy thing were hunting for her through the mists like a shade from between heaven and earth, between past and present, between the world of myth and story and the world in which she shivered on a rock. In mists like this she could be lost in a world of wraiths and spectres. Perhaps she really had died at High Crag Linn and was a wraith herself, roaming the moors for ever.

The hoof beats slowed. The horse had steadied to a walk as if the horseman had found her, and was taking his time, moving in on her.

His face became clear through the mists. She saw Jankin's red hair and beard and the horror in his eyes. *No. No. No.*

The scream came from deep inside her. This time, she would kill him. She raised the stone high and back, and with a cry she lurched forward – but he had turned the horse and was galloping away at full stretch, disappearing into the mists as she stumbled after him.

He was gone. She clutched the stone, her heart pounding hard and her legs weakening. Her shaking was uncontrollable. She staggered back to find Falcon's cloak and wrap it tightly round her.

Sit down, girl. He's gone. Drink some water. She sipped water, but had no stomach for food.

Jankin's gone. Never mind where he is, in earth or hell or in somewhere worse than hell, so long as he isn't here.

But he could come back. Get up, girl! He could come back!

She got up, pulling the cloak around her. Of course he'd come back, he'd only gone to fetch his henchmen! And she was sitting here, soothing herself and sipping water like a lady in a castle! She hung the bag over her shoulder, gathered up the hems of both the cloaks and ran. When she could run no more, she huddled by a rock until she was ready to walk, and walk, and walk; when she could walk no more, she found a sheltered place for a brief, uneasy sleep. As soon as there was light enough to walk by, she dragged herself to her feet, and when her feet felt too painful to walk on, she folded her lips tightly and forced herself forward, holding tree trunks and rocks when she could. She drank at springs and finished the bread. Merciless rain seemed to penetrate through her skin. *I must live. They are all dead, except me, so I must live and tell Anna's story. Whatever Jankin can do, whatever stones and rocks can do to me, I will live.* She remembered Anna's face, the games they used to play, the songs they used to sing – but when she tried to sing the old songs, no sound came out.

Every step she took, she took for Anna. Maybe Anna was watching her from heaven. *Help me, Anna. Pray for me.*

There were sheep on these moors. They must belong to someone. Walking was slower now, her feet being so sore and her legs weakening; breathing hurt. When her legs buckled beneath her, she crawled, until she was looking down into a valley with timbered houses, cattle and smoke rising from chimneys.

Inching her way downhill, she found that down was harder than up. Hunger and poor sleep had left her dizzy and weak enough to lose her footing and fall, tumbling faster and faster onto the sharp stones.

Jankin ordered his men to deface the Lillie coat of arms over the main gate and the hearth. Whose home was this? He stripped down the hangings and flung them across the eyeless holes where windows had been broken. He sent his men to rebuild burned cottages as best they could, scouring the land for timber and stone. There was not a steward or a servant left alive, and nobody from High Crag Tower knew how to run a grand house. They helped themselves to weapons from the armoury and wines from the butts until Jankin locked away the wines for himself.

In Jankin's dreams Anna emerged from the screaming and smoke, melting and twisting like a doll until she was Anna without a face, but still screaming, coming closer to him. She stepped into his dreams as he fell asleep and bent over him as he woke. By day he bellowed orders, growled, pushed and swaggered, driven to fury by the keening that might be the wind in the chimneys or the wailing of the dead, by the half-seen movements flicking before or behind him that might be an effect of sunlight, a shadow on a wall or the taunting of a ghost.

'Why won't they go away?' he growled to Falcon one evening in the solar chamber. Outside, something shrieked. He leapt up, one hand on his sword hilt.

'Do you hear it?' he cried.

'A screech owl,' said Falcon.

Jankin filled his own cup and pushed the bottle towards Falcon, who left it alone.

'The other one still screams,' muttered Jankin. 'Can't ever stop. She's always screaming. I went to the Linn. I saw the footprints. Gey small feet.'

'Aye,' said Falcon. 'She's dead. I made sure of that.'

'They say there's a man down there that saves them.'

'There was no saving that one. I know the difference between dead and alive.'

'She walks, Falcon,' said Jankin. 'Her wraith walks the moors. We'll never be free of her.'

He had seen Thomasin's wraith, her eyes red and wild, her hair and clothes still wet from the Linn, holding up one of the stones she had fallen on, screaming for vengeance. In his nightmares she drew him to the edge of High Crag Linn, inviting him to throw himself down until he could think of nothing else.

The men were grumbling against him, he knew that. They resented his orders, and were slow to obey. When he came near they stopped talking, and he suspected that they were paying more attention to Falcon than to him. That girl, with her spindle and yarn, had been the unravelling of his life. In the mornings he still rode out, galloping through rain to the place where he had seen Thomasin's ghost. She was not there now, but it took all his courage to turn his back on the place.

One morning, he rode back by way of High Crag Linn. He could look down and see if her body still lay in the water, or whether there was a trace of a torn cloak. He should have taken that necklace from her first. It was Anna's, not hers. He dismounted, and gazed down. If he stood there long enough, it was as if the waters roared a summons to him. Let them. He would stand there to defy them, though the longer he stood, the louder they called until their voices filtered into his dreams, and mixed there with the voice of Thomasin. Straggly stemmed birches grew at wild, thrown angles from the rock. The more he looked at them, through morning mist and spray, the more they looked like the white arms of a girl, stretched out for help.

From that time on he rode there every morning, each day stepping a little closer to the edge, bending to look down over the clouds of white water. When rain was heavy, the waters beneath the falls swept all away, living or dead. When the days had been dry the rocks bared their teeth, and were hungry.

The last time he went there, he knew what to expect. The familiar voices would urge him to come. White arms would reach for him. It was as if he needed them. And, away from the falls, what waited for him? Fear of what he would see by night, and fear of treachery by day.

He would not wait for his mind and body to break and for his own men to turn on him. He had insulted Falcon and would not wait for Falcon to stab him in the back, nor for justice to catch him at last and hang him slowly for a crowd's gawping. He would die while he could choose for himself. He would admit to his bride and her shadow that he had wronged them, and this would be his surrender. Then maybe they would have mercy on him, and leave him alone. He stepped firmly to the edge, because he had sent too many men down here to fear it for himself. He decided to leave his sword, so he drew it and left it on the ground, and, as an afterthought, unfastened the sword belt and laid that down, too. *See if you can follow me to hell, wraiths, see if you can still fill my head after this...*

He retreated a few steps, to run at it, and the falls roared for him as he ran. The silver birch arms reached out but they would not catch him, and there was nothing beneath his feet as the rocks rushed to meet him.

'He's not back,' said Falcon. All day, Jankin did not come back. When his horse returned, saddled and alone, they searched, and went on searching until they found his sword on the rocks at the top of High Crag Linn with the scabbard beside it.

It had been laid there neatly, almost with respect, as if a soldier had surrendered it. Falcon lifted it and held it across both hands as if it were a sword of ceremony, a solemn thing, and not a weapon. He knelt at the edge and peered down. Nothing was clear. It was over, then. His boyhood and his loyalty were lost down the Linn. He sat back on his heels, feeling a great heaviness, as if his heart would drag him down after his kinsman.

Chapter Ten

Autumn crept slowly through the cloisters at Hallowburn. Veils of dew and spiderwebs laced the grass in the early light. Leaves deepened to fire and gold, and twirled in the air. Fruit on the trees grew heavy and wasps danced around the windfalls on the wet earth. At matins and compline, sweet voices of nuns rose into the air with the smoke of bonfires and the ripe, warm fragrance of simmering fruit. Anna felt she belonged here.

She slept at nights on a hard bed. She ate barley bread and a kind of porridge. There was meat on Sundays and feast days, and when the nuns fasted, so did she. Because of the burns, she was allowed to wear a soft shift under her habit. Mother Gabriel gave her the name of Sister Penitentia, as she had cried out about her sins when she had been so desperately ill.

She had all she needed. What she yearned for most she could never have again, but the life of the convent was enough. Only Mother Gabriel knew Anna's real name, and she never spoke it.

On a September morning, she walked in the cloisters, slowly, with Mother Gabriel.

'Do you miss your old life?' asked Mother Gabriel.

'My friends,' said Anna quietly. Her speech was still slurred, and she could not yet name Thomasin and her mother without tears. 'I don't miss being the lady and having things done for me, or the clothes.' She managed a faint smile, but only half of her mouth could smile now. 'I don't miss the terrible things, like a cottage being burned when it had contained everything that a family had, and Jankin's men taking the hens the children fed and the house cow that gave them milk, and the lamb that was a child's favourite. I don't miss any of that.'

Mother Gabriel glanced sideways. She caught the quick brush of Anna's fingers against the scarred cheek.

'And your face?' she asked.

'It was only a face,' said Anna with a shrug.

'A very beautiful face, so I'm told,' said Mother Gabriel. 'And a part of you.'

'But I'm not the one who has to look at it!' said Anna. 'It will trouble other people more than it does me.'

'But you keep touching it,' observed Mother Gabriel. Anna whipped her hand away.

'I'm curious about it,' she said. 'It feels strange. I don't exactly miss it, but nobody can like being hideous, whether or not they were beautiful before. It's the people I miss. If I had to choose between my face and my friends, what do you think I would want?'

So this was hell.

Pain had never been far from Jankin, from his father's beatings to the kicks and punches of the fights he had scrapped in as a boy until he had vowed that nobody would ever outfight him again. Whenever he was hurt he would fight back, giving worse than he got. Now, he lay with a sharp stone under his back and rocks all about him, and such pounding pain in his head that he knew he had died from a shattered skull. He had struggled to rise, but lances of pain in his legs felled him and he slumped back, helpless, knowing that the sharp stone was still there and waiting for him to fall on it. As he cried out, pain scorched across his chest.

Hell was being unable to fight back. Nothing to do but wait for more pain.

Somebody was approaching. The demons were coming, and he was helpless. The mercy he had shown in life would be the mercy given to him now. He opened his eyes to a blinding light that made him wince. It could not be sunlight. The sun would not shine in hell. Between him and the light, a face loomed over him.

The demon had a lined, leathered face, dark with age and sun. Keen blue eyes glittered.

Jankin made one last heave to get away, pushing feebly against the rocks, but the pain of the effort made his head swim and his eyes close, throwing him into darkness, nausea and the sensation of falling from dark to darker. As if from far away he heard the demon's voice, softly saying something about getting him to the fire.

Thomasin tried to stand, but falling down the scree had left her torn with grazes, and she was already weak. Her legs buckled. *Then I will crawl.* She twined her fingers into the tough stems of heather and dragged herself forward until she could see the source of the chimney smoke. There was a tree, an ash, standing alone. If she held on to that she could stand, and stay standing, though she swayed and pressed her head dizzily against the bark. Warm, sticky blood was on her shoulders.

A little way off was a large farmhouse with a low surrounding wall and battlements, as if it were something between a castle and a farmhouse. Hearing the laughter of running water, she urged herself on, though as soon as she loosened her grip on the tree she found herself on her hands and knees again.

Near the surrounding wall was a rock. She should sit on that and pull herself together. She couldn't appear at a front door like this, bruised and filthy, and say…

… And say… what?

That was the trouble. If she had never said anything, Anna wouldn't have run away to save Hollylaw. She tried to say, 'My name is Thomasin', but no sound came out.

It might be better not to let anyone know who she was. And who was she? Not the same girl she had been before all this. She sat on the ground, taking deep breaths to clear the pounding and spinning from her head. High, nervous voices of girls reached her.

'Eeh, Alice! Look!'

'Eeh! Get away! Don't go near her!'

'Is she going to die?'

'She might have something catching, so don't you go near her. Do you hear, Sarah? Come away. She's not from here. She's a beggar lass. Eeh, look at the state of her!'

'She's all mucky. Her feet are all blood.'

Thomasin raised her head to look at them. There was a shriek and a scuffle as they drew back.

'She's had her hair cut! That means she's got fever!'

'Eeh, Alice! We should tell Auntie. We should give her something to eat.'

'We'd have to put it on the ground and get away fast. Then maybe she'd eat it and go. Sarah! Where do you think you're going?'

'I'm telling Aunt Joan.' Her voice rose higher as she ran. 'Auntie! Auntie!'

Hoof beats were approaching, beating through Thomasin's head and so terrifying her that her stomach churned and her head swam again. *Jankin has found me. Oh God, have mercy. God protect me, angels and saints in heaven...* But how would Jankin be coming from that direction? The horseman was near – the hoof beats were painful in her head; the rider was coming to the house. When the harness stopped jingling, she raised her head.

A bay horse tossed its head and a young man jumped down. She looked for a sword but he didn't carry one, and had no look of Jankin's men about him. He wore the plain jerkin, breeks and boots of a farmer, and his hair was short and neatly cut. A shriek came from behind him.

'Michael! Don't touch her!'

'No!'

'Please, Michael, she might be diseased!'

'If you touch her you'll *die!*'

The young man squatted down before Thomasin. 'She'll not have anything I haven't caught before, will she? I've seen worse than her. What's your name, lass?'

She must not tell him. She must not be found. She must make something up, say she was Mary or Kate or... but her voice could not make any name at all. It was better to say nothing.

'Where do you come from, then?'

Say nothing. If she told them they would take her back, and Jankin would find her.

He spoke very slowly. He must think she was a simpleton.

'Do you know where you come from? Do you want to go home?'

Home! If she had a voice, she would have screamed, but she could not keep the fear from her eyes.

110

'It's like that, is it?' he said.

Another man was approaching, bigger and older, broad-shouldered and balding with sweat on his round face. There was a likeness between the two – *father and son*, she thought. The two girls squealed something, but he ignored them.

'What's this, Michael?' he boomed. His voice was strong and earthy. 'A beggar?'

'I reckon she's lost,' said Michael, not turning his head from Thomasin. 'Maybe run away. She's scared, that's for sure, and she might be mute for all she's telled me.'

'Aye, well, you haven't the way with the lasses,' said the older man. He bent, bracing his hands on his knees in a way that reminded her of Alan. 'Are you ill, hinny?'

She shook her head. She didn't feel well, but if she said she was ill they might turn her away, and she couldn't go much further.

'Well, if you're not ill, you're hurt,' he said. 'Look at the state of them feet! Look at the state of all of you! Are you hungry, pet?' When she nodded her head, he nodded back at her. 'Of course you are. Michael, don't keep her sitting out here! In the name of all that's good and holy, pet, we'll not see you hungry and heartless, whoever you are. Can you get up? Give us a hand, Michael. God have mercy, she can't stand.' He lifted her as easily as if she were a limp doll. 'There's blood all over you, lass! Now, I'll try not to hurt you. Mistress Joan will get you sorted out.' The two girls gasped with alarm as he strode past them. 'You two, stop squeaking and find your Aunt Joan. Tell her there's company. And I'll hear your news from market, Michael, when we've got this lass settled.'

Chapter Eleven

Thomasin was aware of a wide, clean kitchen, low-beamed, and a woman in a white apron bustling towards her. She had a kind, concerned face, with reddish hair turning to white, and outstretched arms still dusty with flour from bread making. There was a fuss and a flurry in which Thomasin's wounds were washed, she was given a clean shift to put on, wrapped in a blanket, handed a warm posset to drink and, at last, left alone to sip at it slowly and cry quietly at the sudden kindness. The two girls, Alice and Sarah, were still complaining.

'Now, if it were one of you girls homeless and hungry on the moor, wouldn't you want someone to look after you?' said Aunt Joan, and she turned again to Thomasin. 'Now, hinny, you just get that posset down you – it'll do you good. Take your time. You're safe here.' She turned to the younger man, Michael, lowering her voice. 'We'll wait and see if she keeps that down, son, before we give her anything else. Mind, the cat's got her tongue. Now, what's the news from town?'

'Just that everything we've heard from Hollylaw is true, mother, and a lot more besides. There's not many survived. A few got away, a few are trying to scrape their homes back together.'

Thomasin bit her lip. Michael went on, 'That lovely lass is dead.'

'Michael!' cried Aunt Joan. 'You're upsetting the girl!' She put a motherly arm round Thomasin's shoulders. 'Is that where you're from? Hollylaw? Well, you're safe here.'

After that, Michael was careful how he spoke of Hollylaw in front of this new, silent lass. But when he came home from market two weeks later, he thought she would be glad of the news.

'That Hawk Jankin won't trouble the world again,' he said. 'His sword was left by the top of the waterfall. He's put himself down the Linn.'

'Pity he hadn't done it sooner,' said Joan. She knelt beside Thomasin, and took her hand. 'It's all right, pet. Nobody will make you go back there. You're safe with us. That devil's lackey Jankin's dead. It'll be him that hacked her hair off, the evil heathen.'

Thomasin broke down and wept wildly, unable to stop. She wept for Hollylaw, for Anna, for home, for her friends, for Lady Isabel, for Anna, Anna, Anna. And she wept with rage and frustration, because Jankin had chosen his death, and she had kept poison for him.

The first whitening of winter gripped the earth at Hallowburn. The last of the autumn flowers crystallized, thawed and rotted. The narrow window of Anna's cell was etched and leafed with frost. Her damaged skin cracked with the cold and she shivered in her cell, but at meal times the refectory was warm, and she had been set to work in the infirmary, where there was always a fire for the patients. Her mother had taught her about the gathering of healing plants and the making of infusions, salves and poultices, and she learned much more from Sister Agnes, who was in charge of all medicines. Sister Agnes was stern, with a sharp tongue for inattentive novices, a sharper eye for detail and the strictest of standards. The best possible care of her patients mattered to her far more than whether a novice was tired, cold or had not understood instructions – but she made an excellent salve of grease and sheep's wool to soothe Anna's hands.

But nobody called her 'Anna' now. She was Sister Penitentia. Work and the new name helped her to keep the past at a distance. Sometimes, pounding seeds in a mortar and watching them turn to coarse dust, she would forget burning, death, and the castle falling in flames around her. By now she had heard the story of Thomasin's death and had taught herself to face it, but, in her head, she talked as if Thomasin were beside her. It was so easy to think of Thomasin at her elbow, much harder to imagine her dead on the stones at the bottom of the Linn. When a door opened, she expected Thomasin to appear. When a clean habit, shift or towel was placed in her cell it was as if Thomasin had put it there, the way she used to lay out gowns, headdresses and hairbrushes. At compline, she never managed to complete the office without a few tears. At night, she would set her mind to contemplate angels and heaven, because she must not think of Thomasin, dead and broken while the waters splashed over her body and washed the blood from her hair.

She could control her thoughts while she was awake. The nightmares were beyond her, and dragged her helplessly down to fire, the smell of burning flesh, screams and the voice and face of Hawk Jankin everywhere.

Sister Agnes reported to Mother Gabriel that Sister Penitentia showed a real dedication to her work, even – and this might show a lack of humility – taking too much upon herself. She would clean up any filth and treat the most infectious patients. It could be that she was trying too hard to impress.

Anna had decided work was all she had left. She might as well clean up the filth and risk catching diseases. Everyone she loved was dead, so if she died in the course of her work, it wouldn't matter. And, because of her pain and loss, she felt pity for the sick, the helpless, the pained. Her heart went out to the old nuns who had given all their lives, their long ago youth, joy and beauty to this place and were ending their days with burning pains in their joints, weak stomachs and failing sight. It had always been easier to be kind to the young and lovely than to the old, the ugly and the deformed. Anna was ugly and deformed now, and felt sorry for them. She cared for them like children.

She had left her rosary at High Crag Tower, but the nuns had given her another one. On the crucifix she saw a pained, distorted body, like her own, like those of her patients. First there was pity, and then love. She loved her patients.

Jankin believed that he had fallen into hell and a demon had been sent to torment him. While shadows flared by fiery torchlight on the walls, the fiend had steadily tortured and mangled him, and did not even appear to take pleasure in it. His calm face had enraged Jankin.

It was several days before he understood that he had been rescued by Brother Aelred, the hermit of High Crag Linn. Two chambers had been formed in the cliff: a lower one which led by a curving slope to the bottom of the waterfall, and another above it, reached by steps cut into the rock. A brazier warmed it and blackened the ceiling, which the hermit scraped regularly to clean it. An altar had been built in one corner.

By the time Jankin had realized that this was not a devil torturing him but a hermit setting his broken bones and dressing his wounds, the pain was a little less. His shoulder had been so badly shattered that it would never mend cleanly, his broken ribs still left him sore and stiff, and his left arm would hang uselessly for the rest of his life, just as the shattered bones in his hip and thigh would leave him limping – but at least he was not in hell. Hell was there to meet him in his nightmares, but the hermit was always there to wake and soothe him. There was some wooden thing, like a necklace, that the hermit would put into Jankin's hand to grip in pain or distress. When he was lucid, he found that it was a set of rosary beads.

'But I did not give it to you,' said Brother Aelred. 'You brought it with you.'

Jankin looked again, and recognized it. It was Anna's rosary.

He was not in hell, but he could never again be Hawk Jankin of High Crag Tower. What remained for him? The hermit had not asked his name, but he might have guessed it. Unable to walk more than a few steps, let alone run, Jankin resigned himself to spending the winter in this place, hoping the hermit would not betray him.

Kindness was strange to Jankin, and he could not trust it. When Brother Aelred went out he feared that he would bring back soldiers to arrest him. It might be best to kill the hermit, but for now, he was not strong enough to live without his help.

'Why are you here?' he asked the hermit one night.

'Because I am not elsewhere,' replied the hermit simply. 'I was a soldier. Young soldiers exchange tales of killings and burnings, and never ask why. Old soldiers boast less and question more. I would rather heal a man than wound him, so I thought that if God had made me better suited to be a monk than a soldier, then a monk I would be. But it wasn't enough to stay in my friary. I had to serve God in a place where no light shone. This is such a place, and there was already a hermit here, grown old and unable to continue alone. He went to back to the friary to die and I came here, to his hermitage, also to die.'

'To die?'

'Something of us has to die before we can be reborn,' said Brother Aelred.

Jankin grew stronger. Opportunities to kill the hermit came and went, and he let them go. He found himself enjoying the simplicity of life with the hermit. He no longer had the strength to give orders, to ride out, to be better than the rest and to watch for signs of disloyalty, but he no longer needed to. The hermit treated him as a friend. *Poor innocent*, thought Jankin. *What if he knew?*

'The sparrow is trying his broken wings,' observed Brother Aelred one day, watching Jankin lurch awkwardly up the steps with an armful of wood. 'Will he take flight?'

Jankin remembered what anger was. 'Sparrow!' he snarled.

'You fell like a sparrow to the ground, my son,' said Brother Aelred mildly. 'The Gospels tell us that not a sparrow falls to the ground without our God knowing of it. He knows of it, my son. He may not prevent it, but he knows of it.'

Jankin moved his right hand to where a sword should be. 'I was once called Hawk,' he growled. 'Do you know that name?'

'Oh, yes,' said Brother Aelred, gathering up the wood from where Jankin had dropped it. 'I thought it must be you. I had heard your name shouted in curses as your prisoners fell to the stones, many times. Even I had heard of the hawk with the head of fire. And there you lay, with the boots and jerkin of a gentleman, but very well worn. Yes, I knew of you, and knew who you must be. Those I was able to save have long since taken wing. And I think the sparrow – or the sparrowhawk, maybe – might fly too.'

Jankin stepped closer, too close, but the hermit did not retreat. 'I still have a strong right arm,' Jankin said. 'I could kill you now, or I could wait until you fall asleep.'

'I know,' said the hermit, and shrugged. And Jankin laughed, realizing that they were equals. After that the evenings were never too long to talk, to exchange their life stories, to tell of old sorrows and hurts, to learn, to leave the past as he had left his sword. There were months of healing, change and newness. That was the beginning.

Jankin had known that there were men like Aelred, living simply, generously and quietly, but it had never been anything to do with him. The mutterings of priests and threats of hellfire had repelled him. Now, he was discovering something harder than the rocks and more powerful than the Linn, greater than his past and deeper than his heart. The fact that he wanted to change was more astonishing than the discovery that he could.

When Brother Aelred asked him if he had ever been baptized, he had no idea. He supposed he must have been, as an infant. But he had to do something to mark the change in him.

On Christmas Eve, the sky was bright as a sword flash and the air sharp. Jankin stepped naked and goosefleshed into the icy waters of High Crag Linn. The hermit, in his threadbare robe and bare feet, followed him.

The shock made Jankin cry out. The coarse red hairs on his arms bristled, and pain struck through the leg that would always be crooked. The hermit's hands were on his head, and his voice was so powerful that the words rang back from the rocks.

'Do you repent of your sins?'

'I do!' cried Jankin, fighting for breath against the pain and cold.

'Do you renounce all that is evil?'

'I do!'

'Do you turn to Christ?' demanded the hermit, and it seemed to Jankin that all the rocks and the waterfall echoed the response in triumph.

'I do!'

'Then, Jankin, Brother John,' announced the hermit, 'I baptize you in the name of the Father...'

The large, strong hands pressed Jankin down into water so vicious with cold that he felt it would kill him. He rose up, every muscle shivering, his teeth rattling.

'... and of the Son...'

And down into the sharp teeth of the pool again. He opened his eyes, looked down and saw a world of pebble, weed, tiny fish; a new world all about him. Tipping back his head, he saw the dazzle of winter sun through the water.

'... and of the Holy Spirit.'

The stinging waters embraced and released him once more. He rose up laughing with joy at the bright cold sky, his skin tingling. Everything felt new, and free. Shivering and laughing, wrapped in a blanket by Brother Aelred, he returned to the warmth and light of the hermitage.

In the bastle-house at Winnerburnhead, November grew colder and darker. Master Cuthbert Wishart and Mistress Joan began to think of Christmas. The house would be full. As well as Michael, their two married daughters would be with them, and the sons-in-law, and the little grandson, Peter, who was only just finding his feet. Alice and Sarah would not be there.

Alice and Sarah were Joan's two god-daughters. They were the bonniest girls around Winnerburn – brown-haired, rosy and curvy, with deep brown eyes and lashes like hearth brushes – but their mother had despaired of ever teaching them to run a house, and so had sent them to stay at Winnerburnhead in the hope that Joan would train them. The idea that one of them might marry Michael – who would inherit Winnerburnhead one day – was never mentioned, but often thought of.

And, of course the new lass would be with them at Christmas, their – what was she? Maid? Fosterling? She had still not spoken a word, not even to tell her name, but they noticed that if anyone mentioned a neighbour whose name was Thomas, she looked up as if she had been spoken to. Of course, said Joan, the lass couldn't be called Thomas. Tess would do. So they called her Tess, and she came to answer to it.

She was a puzzle. There was nothing of the peasant about her. When her feet were healed and she was well again, she walked gracefully, like a gentlewoman. Her hands were used to skilled work, not soil and farm beasts. She had arrived with two cloaks, one of which was a man's, but the other, once it had been brushed down, proved to be finer than anything in Winnerburn. And that necklace – Joan would have liked a good look at that necklace, but if anyone mentioned it, the girl's hands would fold protectively over it. She even slept with one hand closed over it. Alice and Sarah said she must have stolen it, but then, they would say that. They couldn't resist asking her what man gave her the cloak, either.

'Poor Tess,' said Joan, many times. Thomasin still didn't speak, but she cried sometimes, quietly, without stopping her work. But she was a useful little body, keeping herself clean and neat. She looked for opportunities to be helpful, clearing and washing plates, laying fires without being asked. And as for spinning!

Alice and Sarah had no idea. It wasn't that they couldn't handle a spindle, but they wouldn't, if they could help it. On a day in November around Martinmas, Sarah had left her spindle lying about on the hearth. Joan had been about to scold her when she saw Tess's eyes fix on that spindle like a cat with a mouse.

Joan had lowered her eyes to her work, tying bunches of sage and mint to hang for the winter and layering apples in baskets. She glanced sideways. Tess crept like a furtive thief to the hearth. She had reached out for the spindle, and held it in both hands, looking at it intensely.

What she did next made Joan's heart turn and tears prickle her eyes. Tess had clutched that spindle to her heart and rocked it like a child with a treasure.

By the time the apples were all packed and the baskets put away in the store, the girl had stopped cradling the spindle and taken it to the window, where the light was better. She had teased at the rough wool and rubbed it against her face. Then she had twisted and turned it, a little clumsily at first, until the skill and the rhythm came back to her.

Long forgotten peace came to Thomasin. The wool had smelt and felt like a past she could not recover, but the action was real. She was spinning, and it was as soothing as an old lullaby.

Holy Virgin Mary and Jesus be thanked, thought Joan. *If she's not careful, she might even smile. And what a hand she has with a spindle!*

Thomasin, feeling Joan's eyes on her, had looked up suddenly. She stopped, watchful as a cat, wondering what Joan would say.

'You just spin all you like, Tess,' Joan had said. 'I'll find you a spindle of your own, shall I? There's always fleece that wants spinning here.'

She went to attend to the cooking of a meal, leaving Thomasin at the window, spinning, swaying a little as if to a tune nobody could hear. Then the door creaked open and Alice and Sarah, who had been outside sorting apples, ran in with a fanfare of giggles.

'Michael's home!' called Sarah as Michael followed them in.

'That's my sister's spindle!' cried Alice. She darted across the room, snatched the spindle from Thomasin and smacked her across the face. Thomasin raised her hand.

From behind her, someone caught her wrist and a strong arm locked round her waist. She kicked out viciously behind her, twisted to see her attacker, and looked up into Michael's good-natured face.

'Alice! Tess!' snapped Joan. 'What's this?'

'Little silent Tess!' laughed Michael. 'Stop kicking me! Alice, what did you do that for? Look, you've left the poor lass's face scarlet with your handprint!'

'Good!' retorted Alice. 'She took Sarah's spindle.'

'I don't mind, really,' said Sarah, and she shrank back as Alice turned to glare at her.

'Stop it, all of you,' said Joan firmly. 'Sarah, Alice, just let her spin.'

Thomasin sat still, cradling the spindle. Too many memories had come back when Alice hit her and Michael caught hold of her. She needed to stare at the floor, concentrating on taking deep breaths because otherwise she might not be able to breathe at all, and tell herself that she was safe. It was a relief to know that the attention was on Michael, not on her. Presently Cuthbert, who had been attending to the horse, came in, rubbing his bald head.

'Now, the pair of you,' said Joan, 'any news from the market?'

Michael and his father talked about buying and selling, then moved on to the market gossip of who had prospered and who had not, who was about to marry, who was with child and who had bought land since last market day. Finally, Cuthbert, stretching out his legs before the fire, said, 'And they've sorted out those outlaws at High Crag Tower for good and all.'

'They have?' said Joan. 'About time! Has Sir Hugh Lillie come back?'

They had forgotten Thomasin. She was already sitting so quietly that they did not notice her stiffen.

'No such thing,' said Michael. 'Young Hugh was killed in battle and Sir Hugh was wounded and died of some foul battlefield fever in his wounds. There was some cousin down south who reckoned he had a right to Hollylaw, and as he fought for Lancaster the new king let him have it. He came home to find he'd inherited a burned castle and ransacked lands, with a few of Hawk Jankin's men slinking about like vermin.'

'And sent the lot of them to the gallows, I hope,' said Joan.

'Give us a chance to tell you,' said Cuthbert. 'I heard it from Jock of the Beck, and he was in the fight. After the Hawk ran mad and threw himself down the Linn, his kinsman took over, the one they called Falcon. He held them together for a while, but Jock thinks they were getting ready to disband, leave the tower and go their separate ways before they could get what was coming to them. But the new lord had the edge over them. Rounded up his friends and a few men who could handle a weapon, and took them by surprise. There was a battle that could keep the crows fed all winter. Them that survived the battle were hanged.'

'Including that Falcon?' asked Joan.

'Didn't have a chance,' said Michael. 'Every man wanted to be the one to kill Falcon. They fell on him, but the lord called them off like a pack of hounds and took him on, blade to blade. Jock said it was a right good fight. He's a real nobleman, the new lord, and he got the better of Falcon. Ran him right through. He even sent for a priest for Falcon when he was dying.'

Thomasin clutched the spindle.

'A priest!' cried Joan. 'Why should he have a priest?'

'Wanted one, apparently,' said Cuthbert, and rubbed his head. 'It's never too late to repent, is it, and I reckon he had a fair weight of sins on his conscience. Jock heard him. He couldn't say much at all by then, but he was fighting to get the words out. He kept saying, "Oh, my sin!" over and over as if he wanted to repent, clutching at the new lord's arm and saying, "Oh, my sin!"'

'Tess, are you not well?' said Michael suddenly.

Thomasin tried to say that she would be perfectly well if she could only stop shaking, but it was hard to breathe, let alone speak. She would have dashed from the room, but Joan had run to hold her. Thomasin squeezed her eyes shut and folded her lips tightly, ashamed of her tears.

'She's got fever!' shrieked Alice, dragging Sarah away from her.

'We shouldn't have talked of them things in front of her,' said Joan in a low voice. 'We knew she came from Hollylaw, and God knows what she's been through. It's all right now, Tess, my hinny. Shush, now. That Hawk and Falcon and every evil bird of prey among them. Do you understand, Tess?

Master Cuthbert's friend saw Falcon dead with his own eyes.'

'He did,' said Cuthbert. 'Didn't even live long enough for the priest to get there. Cold by the time they left him, and the crows had found...'

'That's enough!' said Joan, and rocked Thomasin in her arms. 'He's dead and buried, pet, that's all you need to know.'

Thomasin pressed her face against Joan's apron, angry and confused at the sobs that wrenched her. She should not be crying for Falcon, who had killed and burned at Hawk's side. Falcon, who had cared. Falcon, who had died helpless and in pain, trying to say her name.

The next morning, she went to the shed where mounds of apples still waited to be stored. By the time Joan found her, every apple was packed by size and condition, all the baskets were neatly stacked, and the floor brushed clean. Sorting and tidying helped Thomasin. It kept the pain at bay.

They had seen Falcon die. Nobody had seen Jankin die.

Joan marvelled at what a fine lass Tess was, so quick and willing to learn. Where had she learned her skills? Her sewing and spinning were exceptionally fine, and she had a way of caring for clothes and fabrics as if she had worked in a grand place. Joan had tried to trick her into speaking, slipping in sudden questions, but without success. Surprise or pain – such as when hot soup fell on her arm, which may have been Alice's doing – made her gasp, but that was all. Sometimes she cried, quietly, but there was nothing quiet about her rages. If Alice smacked Sarah across the head or Sarah kicked the cat, Tess would fly into such a hitting and scratching fury that she had to be restrained. The Chisholm family down in Winnerburn said that the new girl would speak well enough after a good beating, but Cuthbert and Joan wouldn't have it. Alice occasionally muttered that the girl must be a witch to make everyone at Winnerburnhead take so kindly to her, but not when Joan and Cuthbert could hear her.

In winter, the ground beneath the farm's spring grew slippery with ice. Alice tried every possible way to make sure Thomasin was the one to fetch water when the earth froze. Thomasin made the extra trips in cold, rain and sleet to be out of Alice's way until Joan noticed and put a stop to it.

'Just because she's my god-daughter, Tess, she needn't think she can give orders in my house. I want you to stay in and mend the cloths for Christmas and the curtains for keeping the draughts out. I won't have anyone thinking we're shabby.'

There were moments when Thomasin's memories became so powerful that they washed away everything else. A glimpse of a woman who looked like Lady Isabel or a girl who looked like Anna, a snatch of a song they used to sing, or a neighbour's gossip about Hollylaw would send horrors spinning round her head. Her nightmares would fill with the smell of stale smoke and sweat, darkness and Jankin. He would loom at her to tell her that Anna was dead, they were all dead, and it was all her fault. When she woke, she would find she was crying. Then she would find a corner that needed tidying, leaves that needed raking, or a chest to turn out, and throw herself into a passion of sorting and cleaning. It helped.

Christmas brought Joan and Cuthbert's two daughters, and their noisy husbands. The younger daughter, Beth, was bright and bustling, and the elder, Jannie, was so full of a baby that she could hardly rise from the settle without help. There was Jannie's boy, Peter, Joan and Cuthbert's curly-haired little grandson, thriving on attention and old enough to get into mischief. Thomasin busied herself with scouring and cooking, but none of it shut out the memory of Christmas at Hollylaw with its minstrels and games. The scent of bay and rosemary was both beautiful and unbearable. She put a hand to her necklace now and again, fingering it as if it were a Christmas gift from Anna. She scoured grease from pans until her hands were cracked and bleeding and the old cuts from High Crag Tower stood out livid and ugly.

She avoided the company as much as she could, because laughter was part of a world she could not enter. It was made worse by the sons-in-law, who seemed to think that a girl who could not speak couldn't hear either, and would loudly observe that 'it makes you wonder what she's been through, doesn't it?', and spoke to her loudly and slowly, as if she were deaf or simple. She kept to herself as much as she could.

At the table on Christmas Eve, with Cuthbert tired and heavy-eyed, a son-in-law not knowing when to stop telling his tale and go to bed, Michael out attending to the beasts and little Peter asleep in the crib by the fire, Thomasin had finished fetching, carrying, serving, turning the spit and stirring the wheat porridge. Now and again she glanced at Peter, asleep in his crib. She could not smile, but it was as if something inside her wanted to.

She found she was glad that other people were enjoying Christmas, even if she couldn't. She knew she was making life easier for Joan, and she loved Joan, who had taken her in and mothered her without knowing anything about her. Little by little, quietly, she began to clear the table. Perhaps the company would take the hint and go to bed, and Joan and Cuthbert, who had to be up early in the morning, could go to their bed too. The daughter with child, Jannie, looked desperate for sleep. Carrying broken bread from the table, Thomasin glanced down at Peter in the crib.

Peter was not in the crib. With nobody noticing, he had climbed out, his eyes wide and round as he crawled towards the glowing brightness of the fire.

Thomasin dropped the bread and ran, choking as she tried to speak. The first sound was only a whimper, the second was a rasp, and the third was 'a – a – a!' as she snatched back Peter's outstretched hand and swept him into her arms.

That sound from her own voice hung on the air like unanswered knocking at a door. She felt the hot blush rising in her face and pressed against Peter, folding herself round him for her own protection. It had been a strange, coarse croak, and she didn't wish to repeat it. *Stop looking at me. Please, all of you, stop looking at me.* Joan rose suddenly and finished clearing the dishes, urging her family to their rest, taking attention away from that first, clumsy attempt at sound, but she hugged Thomasin, quickly and warmly, as she bustled past.

Later in the night, when all was dark and quiet and she was sure everyone else was asleep, Thomasin tiptoed to the door. If she could say 'a' to warn a child, she could say 'Anna'. It would be a Christmas greeting to her. She opened the door a little, and turned to face the direction of Hollylaw. Then she drew one deep breath.

'*Anna.*' She whispered the name to the stars.

A soft whimper came from inside the house. Peter had woken, and was crying. Thomasin turned to see Jannie bending awkwardly to lift and rock him. She shut the door, and stepped carefully round the sleepers on the floor.

'Anna,' said Jannie, gently rocking Peter. 'You said "Anna". Is that your name?'

Thomasin shook her head.

'Well, you're a good lass, whoever you are,' Jannie said. 'You're a great blessing to my mam. Shh, shh now, Peter.' She kissed the curls, damp with restlessness, and smiled over his head at Thomasin. 'He'll not settle in a strange place. I think his teeth are bothering him. I don't want everyone else woken up by him.'

Thomasin reached out her arms and, after a moment of hesitation, Jannie handed Peter to her. Steadily, Thomasin walked and rocked him. His eyes grew heavy. His thumb slipped wetly into his mouth and he seemed to sleep, but as soon as she stopped walking the thin wailing began again.

Maybe she should talk to him. 'Anna,' she said. 'Anna, Anna, Anna.' It was the only thing she had said since she came here. Then she knew that she could do the simplest, most natural thing. Singing would be easier than speaking. Pacing the floor, rocking Peter as he grew heavier in her arms, she sang, softly, the carol she and Anna used to sing every year.

> *'Tomorrow will be my dancing day*
> *I would my true love would so chance*
> *To see the legend of my play,*
> *To call my true love to my dance…'*

Her voice quavered and cracked, but she sang. It was a start.

After Christmas Day the company left, and the house became pleasantly quiet. Joan and Cuthbert were gentle and kind, not urging her to say more than she wished to. She had no gift to give and did not expect any, but Cuthbert and Joan gave her one of the hens to be her own and, as promised, a spindle, and Michael brought her a bunch of sweet-smelling rosemary in flower. Thomasin cherished that spindle. Alice and Sarah returned with new gowns, new gloves and sullen faces, homesick for their parents and more than ever ready to take out their bad feelings on Thomasin. 'So she's learned to talk. Well, isn't that convenient.' Out of the girls' hearing, a conversation took place between Cuthbert and Joan.

'Our Jannie wants Tess to go and stay with her, ' said Joan. 'Just to help her until the child comes.'

'But Tess belongs with us!' cried Cuthbert. 'And she's just found her tongue!'

'It's only for a few weeks,' said Joan. 'Just until our Jannie is up and about, then she'll come back. And it'll get her out of Alice's way.'

'I'll miss her,' grumbled Cuthbert.

'Don't you think I will?' said Joan. 'I've become used to having her about. But it won't be for long. And I'll feel easier about our Jannie, having Tess with her.'

The thought of leaving unsettled Thomasin. Nightmares returned, sending her into hours of concentrated spinning and cleaning before she resolved to gather herself together and do what the family asked of her.

Jannie's home was not far away, and Thomasin stayed there for two months. She did the work of the house, cared for Peter, and, when the time came, helped to deliver the baby and held him as he screamed with indignation against the world. And though it distressed her to see Jannie in pain, she felt that she was watching something she already understood – life comes through pain, and cannot come without it. When it was time for her to leave, Peter clung to her, so she found herself promising to return.

For two more years Thomasin stayed with Joan and Cuthbert, leaving now and again to stay with one or other of the daughters if a new baby was due. Every midsummer, when the weather was hot and dry, she fell helplessly into turning out and tidying every cupboard and corner, but, as Joan said, it was a useful habit to have.

Alice and Sarah eventually went home to prepare for Alice's marriage to Watt Chisholm. Watt was a tall, dark man, handsome in a heavy-featured way, reasonable enough when nobody argued with him – and not many people did. The sisters left muttering indignantly about how Joan had always favoured Tess, it wasn't fair, and nobody had ever found out where she got that cloak – a man's cloak – and that expensive necklace. All the same, they left in triumph. The Chisholm family were very prosperous, and would help to find a rich husband for Sarah, too.

By then, it seemed to be agreed by everyone that Tess and Michael should be married. Michael simply and clearly loved her. Joan and Cuthbert had become very fond of her for herself, quite apart from the fact that her household skills would make her a valuable asset to the family. Alice and Sarah were disgusted, but nobody minded that.

Thomasin liked the idea well enough. Michael had been good to her ever since he first found her sitting on the ground in blood and bruises. It often occurred to her that Jankin might still be alive – but he had not found her yet. It would be safe enough to stay here, and truly become part of the family.

She liked Michael, and liking would do. She had never expected to marry for love. If she had ever dreamed of a sweet intense love of woman for man, she had left it behind between Hollylaw and High Crag Linn.

On the night of their wedding she whispered her real name to Michael, because she felt she could not honestly give herself without giving her name. It was to be kept as a secret between them, and he understood.

Love came a year later, with the baby. Thomasin was still gasping and sweating when she reached out to hold him, wrapped him in her arms, and felt that she could never bear to let him go. It was hard to hand him back to Joan to be swaddled and given back to her so that his soft pink mouth could search for her breast. Her heart turned over. Her life now would be filled with joy at all that he was and ferocity at anything that would ever threaten him.

Joan smiled with satisfaction and wiped away a tear. A brave girl, a beautiful bairn, and both of them well. Who could ask for more?

'Michael,' said Thomasin faintly. 'For his father. We'll have to shorten it.'

Chapter Twelve

On Easter morning, after days of powerful spring rain, the water was high under High Crag Linn. The world smelt fresh. Fish flicked and turned in the dapples of the pool. Sunlight filtered through the trees and dazzled on the surface where dragonflies hovered. Jankin watched, taking in every sparkle, every flash of colour and every curve and thorn. He had a pilgrimage to make, and it would be hard to leave this place – but Brother Aelred insisted that Jankin must spend some time training with the Franciscan monks.

'You will learn more than I can teach you,' he had said, 'and live in the community, in the disciplines of the order. Go with my blessing and come back to me, my son.'

Jankin set off to walk there with a satchel and a staff. He considered taking the longer route by way of the moors, where there were bastle-houses, farmsteads and a county town with a priest. They would have offered shelter for a night. But he chose instead to go the direct way, sleeping in shepherds' huts or caves. He could even shelter at High Crag Tower, which was now empty, though it was not a threshold he wished to cross.

He knew the landscape well, and set as hard a pace as he could with the injuries which had left his left shoulder misshapen and the leg on that side crooked and often aching. Two days of hard walking, setting his face grimly against the pain, brought him by nightfall to the nunnery at Hallowburn. The rosy-cheeked nun who received him told him, with motherly smiles, that as a traveller, he was welcome to their hospitality, but as a man, he must be confined to the guest wing, at a distance from the nuns. He heard their voices, though. Singing drifted to him, sweet and strong from the chapel, filling him with peace and the sense of quiet.

'You've come on a good day,' she assured him as she returned, drying her hands on the skirt of her habit. 'It's still the Octave of Easter, so we're keeping a good table. And you'll have company. We have a novice taking her vows tomorrow, so Father Jerome – he's the priest who visits us – is here.' She said nothing more about Father Jerome, but went on, 'I hope you'll remember our novice in your prayers tonight. Her name is Sister Penitentia. I suppose, being a holy brother, you might be allowed to come to the chapel when she takes her vows. I could ask Mother Gabriel. Would you come this way, brother?'

From the cool cloisters, she led him to the guest house and opened the door on to such a glare of heat that Jankin felt his face flush. Sitting by the enormous, blazing fire was a big-boned, swarthy priest who swigged down the contents of a tankard before greeting Jankin in a booming voice.

'Welcome, brother! I'm Father Jerome! Come to the fire and have a drink! Ah, here they come – the sisters!'

A silent grey procession of nuns brought supper and, to Jankin's astonishment, more supper, chickens, beef, cheeses, bread and baked apples until the small table was crammed. Father Jerome dismissed the sisters with a Latin blessing, and slumped on the settle.

Jankin had expected no more than plain bread and beer, and the sight of all that food took away his appetite. At High

Crag Tower, with only rough men, the food had been plain, good, and usually plentiful. With the hermit, it was plain, good, and never quite enough. Sitting as far from the fire as he could, he surveyed Father Jerome, who was feasting wholeheartedly and talking loudly at the same time. Jankin ate plain bread and hot beef and left Father Jerome to work his way through the rest.

'They're good and holy in this place,' announced Father Jerome, wiping grease from his chin. 'They only lay on a spread at Christmas and Easter, and not much then. This is shameful, this. This is no sort of a spread for a festival. You have to go a good way south of here to get a religious house where they keep the feasts properly, with a good table. House full of ladies, this. Too good for their own good!' He laughed until he coughed, repeated his own joke, and refilled his tankard from the large jug of ale. 'They don't bother with a decent wine in honour of Easter. All I can say for this house is, they have a good sister apothecary. Terrifying old dragon of a woman, but a good apothecary. They call her Sister Agnes. Her remedies taste foul, but they work wonders for aching bones and bad stomachs, though the sisters never feed you enough to give you a bad stomach.'

Jankin rose and moved restlessly to the window, struggling for patience. Two years ago he would have slashed this man's neck just for irritating him. He might be a changed man now, but it was hard to swelter in a chamber with a loud, guzzling priest when the night air outside was fresh and clean. Father Jerome went on grunting out his stories of banquets he had eaten and wine he had drunk until Jankin turned suddenly from the window.

'I thought these houses were to offer prayer to God, hospitality to the stranger and food to the hungry,' he said.

'Not to stuff baked meats down the greedy.'

The priest's eyes flared with indignation, but he did no more than slump back in his chair. 'Please yourself,' he said, and rubbed his fat fingers on a napkin. 'Only thought you might like to know where you can get a good meal. You look as if you need one. But maybe you're too holy to eat.'

Jankin reminded himself of something Brother Aelred had said. Life was too small a thing to fill with quarrels. *Make your quarrels light enough to blow away in the wind.*

'Peace be with you,' he said. It was a phrase that covered most things.

The priest shrugged. 'I only came to celebrate mass tomorrow,' he said. 'There's a young nun taking her vows. Then I'm off. The nunnery's the best life for a girl like this one. She's so ugly she wears a veil. Mind, I see some beauties in these nunneries. It's a wicked waste of pretty girls.'

Jankin turned sharply for the door.

'Oh, don't take offence,' said Father Jerome. 'What I mean is, if these families are going to shut a girl away in a convent, they may as well send the ones they want out of the way – stupid ones, troublemakers who are too clever for their own good, the shrews and the ugly ones. And this one's so hideous...' he snorted with laughter, spluttering out the words, '... she has to cover her face so as not to frighten away the visitors!'

He was still laughing as the door banged shut. He shrugged again and reached for another baked apple. Some monks considered themselves better than anyone else. Ate and drank barely enough to stay alive and thought they pissed holy water. This one didn't even have his hair shaved into a tonsure, not even a simple, neat haircut. Nothing but a bedraggled, ginger-haired wreck with a lame leg and a shoulder as crooked as a sickle. And that wasn't a proper sort of monk's rosary at his waist. Father Jerome chuckled suddenly. That was a lady's rosary, and where did he get that from?

Well, let him storm off in a huff like a slighted maid. It was his loss. Father Jerome had intended to tell him about the confession he had heard from the veiled nun. From what he could see, the poor girl had a half-closed eye and skin like birch bark. Must have had some foul disease. So when she confessed to him that in the past she had thought too highly of herself, he had smothered the urge to laugh, and asked her why. She said she – his mouth still twitched as he remembered it – had once thought she could change a violent man by marrying him. Father Jerome's shoulders shook, and he collapsed into helpless cackles of laughter. Had the poor man stopped running yet?

Jankin stood in the cool, fresh air and let it clean away the suffocating heat and the greedy priest. He flexed his injured leg, and rubbed the shoulder which was aching badly. The presence of Father Jerome in this place was like a fat slug in an orchard.

He thought of what Brother Aelred would say, and was ashamed. Who was Jankin to criticize anyone? *Anna, Flower of Hollylaw, what have I done?* He raised his face to the sky, and his eyes blurred. *Anna. If only I had died, and not you.*

Tonight, in this holy house, he would pray for Anna's soul and for Hollylaw. He would leave early in the morning rather than stay and defile this place with his rough presence, but he would pray for Hallowburn and the Sisters of the Magnificat. *Anna, if only I had loved you, courted you, won you, for yourself, and not for Hollylaw.* But Anna was dead, and 'if only' led him nowhere.

A light moved along the cloister. Two nuns were gliding side by side, and he turned to leave them in peace, noticing that one of the two wore a veil over her face. This must be the nun who was to take her vows. He resolved to pray for her too.

Anna, if you hear me from heaven, I am truly sorry. Please forgive me. Pray for me. And please pray for this young nun at Hallowburn.

Mother Gabriel escorted Anna to her own chamber and indicated to her that she should sit. It was growing cold, and Anna wriggled her hands into the sleeves of her habit.

'Sister Penitentia,' said Mother Gabriel, 'I told you that it might not be a good idea to confess all to Father Jerome. I don't think he is as discreet as he should be. His silence may not be trusted, but you know that mine can. Is there anything you still have to tell me?'

Anna twisted the hem of her veil, and remembered that fidgeting was discouraged. And as Mother Gabriel knew what she looked like, it was a relief to lift back the thick white linen and feel the freedom to speak face to face.

'Many times,' she said, 'I've blamed myself for what happened. My mother would have taken a sword to her own heart before she'd have let him near me. She warned me what sort of an overlord he'd be, if Father and Hugh didn't return. I thought I could at least buy time until they *did* return…'

She shrieked. A draught was making the candle flare, and her hands flew to her face. Behind her closed fingers, she saw fire.

She never knew when these attacks would come upon her. They were always cruelly sudden, when she had not been thinking of fire and pain and battles. They would leap out before her: the hellish roar and crack, the smell, the screams, the greedy ogres of flame, arching and rearing, and the girl – the girl she had given her necklace to, telling her to get out, to get the children out and get the necklace to Thomasin… the beam had fallen – she had cried out to warn the girl, she had tried to reach her, but the flames… she had dropped her dagger… somebody had held her back. That was all.

Mother Gabriel was speaking, soothing her. Anna forced herself to breathe deeply and slowly. Sweat soaked her hands and prickled her scarred skin. She knelt to press her hot palms on the floor, then on to her face. The shaking would stop soon.

'When you are ready,' said Mother Gabriel.

Anna waited until she had finally breathed out the fear and fire and found the peace of the quiet room with its crucifix and plain furniture. She found her voice again.

'I believed that if I wed him, I would change him,' she said. 'All my life, I had been told how special I was. I was the Flower of Hollylaw. I thought I could just bring goodness wherever I went. I thought I'd bring goodness and peace to Jankin. I was young and foolish enough to believe all the nonsense they told about me.'

Mother Gabriel did not try to blame or to excuse her. She only said, 'And do you forgive the deluded girl that you were?'

'Oh, yes,' said Anna. 'She meant well, the girl I was then.'

'Is there anything else that needs to be forgiven?'

Anna wondered what she was expected to say. She had learned, slowly, to forgive Jankin. She had found that she needed to forgive her father for taking Hugh and the fighting men away and leaving them unable to defend themselves. Forgiving the kings and noblemen who made wars was harder.

'Have you truly, fully, from your heart, forgiven Jankin?'

asked Mother Gabriel. 'Even when the flames leap before your eyes again, as they did just now?'

'I think so. How can I be sure of it? I'll never have to meet him again; I'll never have to face him.'

'He had Thomasin killed,' said Mother Gabriel.

Anna squeezed her eyes shut. *Thomasin.*

'When I think of that,' she said, struggling against everything in her that strained and stung and tried to cry, 'I tell myself that he was a little child once, and little children don't bring themselves up. Something went wrong. And he died a wretched death.' She had to speak quickly, while she still could speak, and the words tumbled over each other. 'There has to be forgiveness, because otherwise there'd be nothing good, nothing bigger than what he did, and he would have won. As far as I know, Mother, I've forgiven him, and I'm as sure as I can be that I mean it, and that's the best I can do. But I can't forgive myself for being the one who lived when they all died.'

'That,' said Mother Gabriel, 'is God's affair, not yours. Let it go.'

Anna was to spend that night in the chapel, at prayer on front of the altar before taking her vows. She prayed for the souls of the dead, especially for Thomasin and her mother, even for Falcon and Jankin who had died so much in need of prayer. She prayed for the sisters in the nunnery, the sick in the infirmary, the visitors in the guest house; about her the nuns processed in, sang the offices and glided back to their cells.

Before sunrise, she lowered the veil over her face and slipped back to her own cell, huddling against the cold of the dark morning. One of last night's visitors was already on his way, lurching crookedly on a lame leg. Knowing what it was to be slowed and pained by old injuries, she raised her one good hand, and prayed a blessing over the pilgrim hobbling away towards the hills.

Chapter Thirteen

Midsummer brought prickling heat – stinging, itching and painful to Anna. Long sunny days and harvest haunted her with terrible memories. With all her strength she concentrated on her work assisting Sister Agnes, though sometimes she would shake so much that a dish would drop from her hands or a medicine spill across the table, and Sister Agnes would scold her as if Anna were a scullerymaid. In time, the memories grew less and her skill grew more. Autumn came, and long, weary hours of drying, bottling and preserving. Winter filled the infirmary, then it was spring, and midsummer again, and every season carried her further away from Hollylaw and the past.

Jankin spent two years at the monastery and, by the end, he yearned for the high airy moors, the wildness and the waterfall. He had learned much, but the hard winter had left him with a painful cough which would not go away, and there were mornings when his breathing hurt terribly. He supposed that his fall down High Crag Linn had wrecked his lungs as well as his limbs. He set himself the fastest pace and the longest hours of walking he could endure, until he reached the spring moor and heard, far off, the voice of the waterfall; there was the joyful, welcoming call of Brother Aelred, meeting him with the outstretched arms of a father.

At the monastery Jankin had assisted the bee-keeper, and found that, as his withered left arm had no sensation, stings had no effect on it at all. He took to bee-keeping as readily as if he were born to it, and from High Crag Linn he set beehives on the moors. In all seasons the hermit and his helper ventured out to visit the nearest dwellings, to give help where it was needed and to pray over Hollylaw. The shepherds and tinkers of the moors became their friends. Houses in Hollylaw were being rebuilt, but Jankin rarely went there. He was lame and deformed, his arm had withered, his hair had darkened over the years, and he looked leaner and older – but he did not like to risk being recognized. Nobody would trust him if they knew who he was, and he enjoyed being trusted, loved, welcomed and asked to help. For the first time in his life, nobody was afraid of him.

On a summer morning, as he made his way down from the beehives, the moors hummed with bees and exhaled heather and bracken. He fell into step with a tinker, a dark, sturdy man with a broad hat, stout boots, a pack horse at his side and a great, bulky pack on his back. Like most tinkers, he was a ready talker, and they sat down on a rock together to share bread and beer, swatting the flies away as they ate.

'What have you to tell me?' asked Jankin, brushing crumbs from the brown habit he now wore.

'Not much,' said the tinker. 'Usual bouts of summer sickness round about, nothing serious. Least I don't think so. Trade's good. Just been to Winnerburn, and Winnerburn market's thriving these days. There's good money round there. The Chisholms never miss a chance to make money. Young Watt Chisholm and his wife have a little lass now.'

They talked of local folk, local affairs and the likelihood of bartering honey and goods on the tinker's return. Soon the tinker walked on, wanting to cover as much ground as he could, still thinking of Winnerburn market. Now he came to think of it, that lass at Winnerburnhead, Michael Wishart's wife, had a look of someone he'd met before, someone from around here. Hang him if he could remember who.

The summer sun grew stronger, hotter, rising early and setting late in flying banners of red over the moors and the farmsteads of Winnerburn. At the Wishart farmstead at Winnerburnhead, the harvesters went out in broad hats and white shirts against the sun. Stone jars of cider and ale were never far away.

Thomasin lay awake at nights, short nights that were too long for her. Michael's steady breathing beside her made her envious and irritated, but sometimes she would lay her head against his shoulder for comfort. She had moved Cal's truckle bed – Cal, short for Michael – from the end of their bed to her side, and lay with one arm touching his small hand. If Michael snored she would turn restlessly, because she needed to hear Cal's breathing, in case it stopped. Sometimes she believed it really had stopped, and would sit up in alarm, pressing her fingers against his neck, feeling for a pulse, waiting for a sigh or a snuffle.

Summers were her worst time, when the past, like the sun, was at its strongest. She would throw herself into the harvesting or into clearing out the chests, scrubbing, cleaning, scouring, pounding linen in a tub until sweat made her gown stick to her, spinning when the light faded. She wrapped her love around Cal and fastened it tightly. He must wear his hat and his white shirt against the sun. She cleaned with vinegar and hung up mint and tansy because these were the things that kept diseases away. Cal must drink fresh water straight from their own spring and the newest milk from their own cows. He must always be within her own sight, or Joan's, or Michael's, in case he fell into the river or wandered off and was lost. Whatever she was doing, however furiously she scrubbed and cleared and changed the rushes on the floor, she constantly glanced up to see where he was.

What if Jankin were still alive? What if he found me? If he killed me, Cal would be motherless, and I must not leave little Cal motherless. And if he found Cal... oh, God, may Jankin be truly dead. She had kept the little flask of poison in a recess in the wall above their bed, very high, where Cal could not reach it.

'Our Tess is in a state,' Cuthbert would observe at these times.

'Let her be,' Joan would reply.

'Whole house smells of vinegar. She's even put mint under the mattresses.'

'Let her get it out of her system, whatever it is,' insisted Joan. 'It was summertime when Hollylaw was sacked.'

Alice had moved to the growing town of Winnerburn, and Sarah, newly and sullenly married, had moved in with her widower husband – Robert Foster, old enough to be her father, wealthy and childless – to the other side of the valley at Winnersmoorfoot. Her first pregnancy made her sick and wretched.

Alice was on her way to being a grand lady of the community. The Chisholm family made the best cheese in that part of the county. Alice turned up her nose at the work of making cheeses, but she was so good at selling them that they were said to fly from the market stall.

Alice appeared to have had all she wanted. Watt Chisholm was a good match with far and away the best cattle for miles.

He could afford to employ maids in the dairy and the house, and to keep a beautiful wife who cared more about her gowns than her kitchen – and Alice, who had never liked hard work, suddenly realized how much money she could make by it and set to wrapping, storing and selling cheeses as if it were a charm against the evil eye.

She gave birth to a little girl, Philippa. 'What have they called her? PHILIPPA! Must be after Alice's father, he's a Philip. Eeh, but Philippa! That's a gentry name. Who do they think they are?' Fortunately little Philippa looked like her mother, not her father.

In the first few months of her life, Philippa had mild spasms and twitchings that sent Alice screaming to her mother or to Joan, but Philippa always recovered quickly. Then, on a warm spring day when Philippa had played happily all morning and fallen asleep in her mother's lap outside the farmhouse, she had transformed without warning into a jerking, gurning, twisting monster.

It was by far the worst fit Philippa had ever taken and the last, but it left her changed for ever. Alice consulted her mother, her Aunt Joan and the priest. More discreetly, with money handed over and nobody to see, she consulted a woman who was said to have forbidden powers. Nothing worked. For the rest of her life Philippa would carry one shoulder higher than the other and her head a little forward and to one side, her right arm fixed and immoveable, her smile lopsided.

Lying awake, night after night, Alice thought that if Philippa had been born like that she could never have loved her. Every day she saw in her mind the lovely, chestnut-haired, blackberry-eyed little princess that Philippa had been and the village beauty she would have become. She still loved

Philippa fiercely, but she needed someone to blame. When she miscarried her second baby, she took to her bed and would not be comforted.

'I must be cursed,' she thought. 'Somebody has ill wished me.' Slowly, it began to make sense.

Tess had intruded into all their lives, and none of them knew where she had come from. For months she had not spoken, but when she did, she'd not told them a thing about her past. But everyone loved her. Joan had preferred the incomer to her own god-daughters.

That Tess had captivated them all just by twirling a spindle. She had even made Michael fall in love with her. What could it be but witchcraft? And more witchcraft, too, so that nobody had noticed what she was up to. They didn't even know her real name.

She had that necklace too. Maybe it was the devil's gift to her. It was too good a thing for any ordinary girl. She had sometimes woken screaming in the night; that must mean something. And Alice had sometimes seen her, when she undressed, slipping something silver into her hand. It looked like a flask of something, but she never got the chance to see what. And…

Alice sat up in bed and hugged her knees. She'd often seen the scarred, lumpy skin on Tess's forearms. A shiver ran down from the back of her neck. *Devil marks, for suckling imps.*

Excitement thrilled through her. The lying, designing, cunning witch, smiling and smiling behind her hand at all of them! By witchcraft she had won Michael. And as for the child! That corn-haired, violet-eyed little boy was not earthly. He was a devil's spawn, and Tess was the foulest witch that ever cast an evil eye, muttered a charm, cursed a child or drowned in a river.

Alice would weave a web that would leave no way out for the stranger, the witch who had put the evil eye on Philippa. She would pass the thread to her sister, her mother and father, and her neighbours, and let them all spin it. There were plenty of girls who envied Tess of Winnerburnhead her home, her husband, her son, her skill, her undeserved luck. They'd all help.

In the next two weeks, the young mothers of Winnerburn fretted and worried, as sicknesses came with the hot weather. There were fevers, especially among the children. 'Makes you wonder why,' Alice would say, with a glance towards Thomasin.

When the tinker next met Jankin, sweet amber honey was exchanged for fleeces that would keep the two holy brothers warm in winter. Again they shared bread and beer, though this time the tinker wondered if Brother John was choking on crumbs or simply had a bad cough these days.

'It's awful dry over yon side, Winnerburn way,' remarked the tinker. 'Some nasty fevers round there.' He drew the back of his hand across his mouth. 'I telled them, it's the market. That market's getting bigger and bigger. I reckon all places have their own diseases, but with a market town, you never know what's coming in with the stock and the buyers.' He glanced sideways at Jankin. 'Not like me, I'm the local tinker – it's part of my parish, you might say. But there's many come to market might be bringing diseases with them.'

'How is Hollylaw?' asked Jankin.

'It's getting itself on its feet,' said the tinker. 'They'll not get diseases there – not enough folk go there to bring them in. Him at the castle, the new lord and the lady, they have no time for tinkers, but I sold to his servants. Not like the old days.

Lady Isabel knew what she wanted. She chose all her lace and ribbons herself, or she'd send that young lass, the maid. She was young, but she... now, there's a thing!'

He stared ahead of him with such a fixed expression that Jankin looked to see what had caught his eye. There was nothing. He waited.

'That's it!' the tinker exclaimed. 'Well, Michael and All Angels!'

He seemed to be pausing on purpose, so Jankin would respond. Jankin waited.

'There's a lass at Winnerburn,' said the tinker finally. 'I always knew she had a look of someone. She's the living spit of the Flower's maid that was at Hollylaw, God rest her.'

Gooseflesh made the hairs stand up on Jankin's arms. The back of his neck prickled with cold.

'Who's this lass at Winnerburnhead?' he asked, and tried to sound casual.

'Married the Wishart lad,' said the tinker. 'Busy, solemn little thing. Don't know her name, except it'll be Wishart. Has a little lad.'

Jankin took care to speak steadily. 'I heard the maid from Hollylaw was thrown down the Linn,' he said.

'Who? Oh, her. Oh aye, she was,' said the tinker. 'That pig's runt Falcon, if you'll pardon me, Brother, he did it because Hawk Jankin hadn't the stomach to do it himself. And that lassie has such a look of her, you'd take her and the maid for sisters. I tell you, brother, I don't know who the maidservant's father was, but I reckon he crossed the moor more than he should.'

Jankin laughed because he was expected to, but his chest felt tight. He worked through the day as he always did, carrying water for a young woman too overwhelmed with the care of her little children, her fields and her home to do all that needed doing, visiting a family mourning their child and praying, long and silently, for the healing of Hollylaw, looking forward to his return to the waterfall at the end of the day. It was a warm, sweet-scented evening, the sort of evening when lovers should be whispering promises and exchanging love tokens, when the beasts could graze lazily and the fiddler play in the streets just for the joy of it. Stars were rising in a pale sky when he took the cliff path down and clambered across the rock to the stone chamber.

'Peace be with you, Brother John,' murmured Brother Aelred.

'And with you,' said Jankin. 'Brother, I need to ask you something.'

'Ask, then,' said Brother Aelred peaceably. 'But first take water for your throat.'

'It'll do no good,' muttered Jankin. He had grown accustomed to his injuries and the pain they still brought him – they were like battle scars – but hoarseness and coughing seemed like a weakness. Sometimes, especially in the early morning, his breathing sounded like the wheezing of an old man, and he despised it.

'Brother, a little while before you found me,' he began, 'there was a girl.' His throat tightened again, as it always did. 'About – I can't remember – maybe a week, or two weeks, before I came here. Falcon threw her down the Linn.'

'Did he?' queried the hermit. He sounded genuinely surprised.

'Don't you remember it?'

'There were many broken bodies at the foot of the Linn in those days,' said Brother Aelred. He gazed absently ahead, as if leaving his gaze in the air while he searched his memory.

Jankin tried to be patient, and failed.

'Please, Brother,' he said. 'I know there were many, but this was a girl. Young.' Brother Aelred still did not respond and Jankin dug painfully into his memory, searching for Thomasin. 'Dark hair, curls. Slender… Falcon cut her hair. Shorn hair, but there must have been curls left.' And there was a necklace. That cloak of Anna's, what colour had it been? What colour had Thomasin been wearing? Grey as a ghost? Grey, torn and dirty, after her imprisonment. There was no point in trying to hurry Brother Aelred.

'No,' said the hermit at last. 'I do not remember seeing such a one, and I think I would have remembered. But if I had been away on my travels, the waters could have washed her away without my knowing of it. Sometimes, as you know, the victims were thrown from the cliff a little further on, and were washed downstream. And even here, if the Linn was full, bodies did not always stay long.'

'Any shorn curls?' demanded Jankin. 'Any shreds of a woman's garments?' He raked his memory. 'Shoes, she wore shoes, they would have fallen off. It was a dry summer, she wouldn't have washed away! The water was low!'

'I saw no sign of her,' said the hermit firmly. 'That does not mean, Brother John, that she was not thrown down the Linn. It simply means that I did not see her.' He jerked with astonishment as Jankin grasped his shoulders.

'Then she might have lived!' cried Jankin, and light shone in his eyes. 'Falcon brought me her hair, but he could have cut it and let her go!'

Brother Aelred had regained his calmness. 'Would that be typical of him?'

'No, it would not,' said Jankin. 'He was like me. He'd tip them over and turn away with a shrug. He'd walk away laughing. But she was young, Brother. Even Falcon might have pitied her! And it was up to him. She was…'

The man he had been disgusted him. He said it quickly, to get it over.

'I promised him he could have her if he wanted her. It was the way we did things. The lady was mine, the maid was Falcon's. But the point is, Brother, she might have lived! Maybe he let her go, God have mercy on his soul. Maybe he cheated me for her sake! The tinker told me that there's a young woman at Winnerburnhead who looks like her!'

Brother Aelred looked at Jankin with his head on one side until Jankin felt that all he had said was ridiculous. All he had was a shred of tinker's gossip. Even if Falcon hadn't killed her, it didn't mean that she'd settled down at Winnerburnhead. As the tinker said, maybe Thomasin's father had taken his pleasures with some woman on the north side of the moors. It seemed likelier than compassion from Falcon.

'Did Falcon show any attachment to the girl?' asked Brother Aelred gently.

'Never showed…' then Jankin stopped.

'She's just a lassie.'

'He asked me to spare her,' he said. 'When I first wanted her dead, he claimed the right to spare her. She cried.' He stared at the ground. He would not know what to say to Thomasin if he met her. No doubt she thought he was dead. It was better that way.

'I just want to know,' he said lamely. 'I want to know if she's alive. I did think once that I saw her ghost. But my mind was wild in those days, and I don't know what I saw.'

Brother Aelred watched a brown trout wind through the pool below them.

'There are reports of sickness round about Winnerburn,' he

said. 'It is not a place we generally visit, but I suspect that they are not well served by any priest. It might be wise to go there. Even, perhaps, to make your way out to Winnerburnhead, wherever that is. If you are strong enough, maybe you should go.'

'I'll go in the morning,' said Jankin.

'Empty-handed? What use will you be, if they need help? In the morning, go to the nunnery at Hallowburn. Greet the ladies of the house, go to the sister apothecary and ask for medicines. Take them honey.'

Winnerburn was such a grand place these days, and the Wishart place at Winnerburnhead was thriving. The sheep and cows were healthy and well fed, the fleeces were strong and clean. On summer days, white linen aired over sweet-scented lavender and rosemary bushes. Young Tess had a neat hand with everything. On market days she stood out with her spotless gown – plain russet, same as everybody else's, but always well cared for. And that little lad was lovely, his hair always clean and brushed, his frocks so beautifully stitched.

The whispers spread like disease in apples.

When Sarah made a scathing remark about Tess, Alice hushed her quickly and looked around as if to make sure nobody was listening. 'Take care. You don't want anything to get back to her. Do you want anything to happen to your baby? Look at mine.'

Winnerburnhead's beasts stayed well when others were sick. Poor Alice's little Philippa had been stricken and she'd lost the next baby, but Tess's Cal was so fair that he turned heads in the market. And wasn't it a strange thing, the way Michael had fallen for Tess? Alice and Sarah were beauties with dowries to bring with them, but Michael had fallen for that penniless mouse. *(Is she such a mouse? Sarah says she has an awful temper on her, like a wild thing, if something sets her off.)* She only has the same hours in the day as the rest of us – how come she manages to do everything so well?

'She never says a word about herself. Alice says she has such a fine necklace, and won't tell where she got it. Do you think she stole it and ran off?'

'Do you know, she'd been to Alice's house just before the bairn had that terrible fit?'

'She'd been looking at my old ewe, the day before the poor beast broke a leg.'

'Sarah and Alice said she had a little bottle that she used to keep hidden in her clothes or high up on a shelf. She didn't know they knew about it.'

'They said sometimes she'd just stop what she was doing and freeze, or shake. Makes you think.'

'Tess is a nice girl, but she does keep to herself.'

'I always thought she knew more than she was letting on.'

'She and Alice never got on.'

'She carried a grudge against Alice.'

'Look at that poor wee Philippa.'

'She has a wonderful way with her sewing and spinning.'

'She has tricks with her sewing and spinning.'

'She has some help we don't know about.'

'Who knows what Michael sees in her?'

'There must be something that attracts him.'

'She must have a power we don't know of.'

'Sometimes she shivers and turns white, as if she were terrified.'

'As if she were touched by the devil.'

'And maybe she is.'

'You know, I was talking to you yesterday about that Tess

from Winnerburnhead? Well, last night the fox got in among my chickens.'

Chapter Fourteen

Angelica. It was one of Anna's favourite scents, and today it was all round her. For days she had worked with the sharp, medicinal aromas of rosemary and thyme or the earthiness of chamomile and feverfew, which she didn't like. But now the angelica must be harvested, and she had been out before dawn to gather it before the flowers lost their potency. It was a sign of Sister Agnes's approval that she had allowed Sister Penitentia to prepare the angelica, because it was no common herb. She had left her to do it unsupervised too, because it was Sister Agnes's turn to keep vigil before the altar, so Anna was alone.

Outside, sunshine baked the gardens, but the stone shed was always cool, pleasant and airy. Sunlight through the open door cast bright shafts of warmth onto the flagstones. Today there were no medicines to be made and no grease to be melted, just summer air and the fragrance of angelica. Anna loved days like this.

When she had first worked in the hospital, she had felt that every injury she healed, every life she restored and every pain she quelled was something won back from the wreck of Hollylaw. Now she hardly thought of Hollylaw except in summer, when the heat and any passing mention of what had happened still made her withdraw to the apothecary's room and be as busy as possible. If that did not keep the spectres away she would let the pain overwhelm her, and when she had finished crying she would light candles for Thomasin and Lady Isabel and return to her work. But her best hours were the early summer mornings in the garden, the shared singing of the nuns in chapel, the quiet night hours holding the hand of a patient by candlelight. And there were harvests of sweet, fresh lavender, rose and marigold, and the moments when a sister nun would see her without her veil and not be dismayed. When Anna thought of Jankin and Falcon and their crew, she thought of them as children who had been given poison in their thinking and their hearts, and who had grown corrupted by it. She tried to see them as the little children they once had been.

Imagining them as children made her think of babies, and that was a deep sorrow. There would never be a baby to smile into her face, play with her hair, fall asleep in her arms and love her. Well, it was the same for many women. Life here was good enough.

A shadow in the doorway made her look up, and quickly lower her veil at the sight of the young novice, Sister Hild, round and sensible, standing in the doorway, holding a bowl in her hands. She had turned pink, and was looking down at the bowl with determination. Anna pretended not to know that Sister Hild had seen her without her veil.

'Please, Sister Penitentia,' said Sister Hild shyly, 'we have a visitor. Mother Gabriel says Sister Agnes can't be disturbed, so I was to send him to you, but it's all right, sister, he's a monk. He's going off visiting and healing and he wants some medicines, and look what he's brought us!'

She held out the bowl, and Anna lifted the cloth. Waxy honey glowed in the dish.

'Mother says I'm to take it to the kitchen and we're all to

have some on St Peter's Day,' she said. 'She thought Sister Agnes might want some for medicines.'

'I'm sure she will,' said Anna. 'Where is this visitor?'

'Mother said he was to wait for you in the herb garden,' said Sister Hild. 'And she would like some fresh lavender, please.'

'Thank you Sister, peace be with you,' said Anna. She rubbed her hands on her habit and went out to the sunny garden. There he was, a man looking up to admire the apple trees, but his posture was awkward – perhaps he had a hunched back. As he turned and saw her he limped towards her, and her heart went out to him. He was probably in pain.

'Sister Penitentia?' he asked, and bowed. 'Peace be with you.'

His voice was familiar, but it could not be. Not the voice of one of the visiting priests – that rough breathiness was wrong. Thyme and coltsfoot came to mind, she should offer thyme and coltsfoot – if only she could get that out of her head, she might be able to recall where she had heard this voice before.

'Peace be with you,' she murmured absently. He was coming nearer, introducing himself.

'I am Brother John, the companion of Brother Aelred of High Crag Linn…'

The name of it made her gasp. And he was nearer. Something was beating in her ears. Dimly through the veil she saw his face and flame leapt before her eyes.

'Sister?' he said in concern.

She managed one step back. Two steps, before the trembling overcame her. *Scream. Call Mother Gabriel, call Sister Hild…* But her voice would not come, and nobody was close. Her hands shook, her legs, her stammering lips – he had found her, the dead man was not dead, the safe place was not safe, this time the nightmare was real and she would not wake up…

Jesus, have mercy…. Ave Maria, gratia plena…

'Sister!' he said again. Why was he calling her 'Sister'? She must not fall. He was nearer. She held out her hands to keep him away – but he had run past her and was shouting as he used to shout his demands across the moat at Hollylaw.

'Sister Pentitentia is unwell! Bring water! Bring Mother Gabriel!'

Anna sank to the ground and put her hands down – better to sit than to fall, she told herself. Sister Hild was running down the path, shielding the bowl of water in her arms to keep it from slopping.

'Should we get her to the hospital, Brother? Should I fetch Mother Gabriel?'

Jankin ignored her, dipping the edge of Anna's veil in the water, lifting it back to bathe her face and hold the bowl to her lips.

'Drink this, Sister,' he said.

The bowl fell from his hand.

Scarring ran across the earth-and-leather skin, but one eye was still blue and long-lashed. The other was half closed with a crinkled and drooping lid, like a dead thing.

He must be mistaken. He had seen Anna dead, and now he was distressing this poor ugly nun by staring at her scars. He looked down instead at her hands, still shaking in her lap, stained with sap from the plants, and the left one… He turned his face away from the sight and heard her whispering her prayers in Anna's voice.

There was a fault in the speech which had not been there before, but it was Anna's voice, just as it was Anna's ruined face, with fear in the one clear blue eye. Here, clearly and close enough to touch, he saw what he had done to every man, woman and child in Hollylaw, to the village, to everything he had touched in the old years. Whatever he could say to her, it would not do.

He might be a ghost, thought Anna. She traced a shaky cross in the air and whispered a prayer to send the unholy thing away. No, he was still there.

'You were dead,' she whispered.

'I should be,' he whispered back, and reached for her hand, but she drew it away. 'I am not what I was. What you see is what I am. I am so sorry, Anna.'

The name made her flinch. She had still not found her voice when the sisters gathered around her to help her back to her cell, assuring her that she was simply suffering from the heat, leaving Jankin to seek out Mother Gabriel.

In the coolness of her cell she lay silent and shaking, hugging herself because there was nobody else to hug her. Jankin was alive. She said it over and again like a prayer on the beads, until she could breathe deeply and say it slowly.

Jankin is alive.

Shh, now. She soothed herself as Thomasin would have soothed her. *He's changed. He's changed.*

Has he? Could he? Could he ever really change? Perhaps he had, but he had deceived her before. She had forgiven him, believing him to be dead. Now she had to forgive him alive, and that would be harder.

She rubbed a clammy hand down the skirt of her habit, tried to sit up, and felt dizzy. She would have to stay still and calm herself to gather strength, because now she had to do the impossible. She had to treat him as the man he now claimed to be.

At last she insisted that she was well enough to go back to her work. She must speak to Brother John herself, to make sure he had exactly what he needed for his travels. No, there was no need to send for Sister Agnes. In the herb garden, she heard Jankin's story and told her own.

'Anna – Sister,' he said, 'I have hated the burning of Hollylaw ever since I did it. I have changed. I am so sorry, Anna. I have repented, truly and thoroughly, but believe me, Anna, never as much as I do now, when I see your face. I…'

'My face!' The composure of the nun fell away. 'My face! Didn't you see enough burned bodies? Didn't you see the children, running and screaming with their clothes on fire? I still see them! What about the girl I gave the necklace to? How badly was she burned, if you took her for me?' Tears gulped in her throat and hurt her. 'What about Thomasin? You burned Hollylaw in a rage, but you weren't fighting a battle when you handed her over to Falcon! And you dare to tell me you're sorry because of my face!'

She was quivering with rage. Jankin tried to think of something to say, something that would help, but could not. He dropped to his knees, vulnerable as a naughty child, and tried to think of words to say. There were none.

Anna had found his words hard to believe, but she believed his silence. It was no good scolding like an indignant market woman, telling him that sorry was not enough, and would not change anything. It was all he had to offer.

He seemed smaller than she remembered him. He had no leather jerkin now, and no sword, only a hunched shoulder that must pain him. She had never met Brother Aelred of High Crag Linn, but he had the reputation of a truly holy man. Perhaps he really had brought grace to Jankin.

'Get up,' she ordered. 'Why Thomasin? Why did you have to kill Thomasin?'

'I feared her,' he said. For now, that was all he could say.

She could understand that. She remembered all she had

ever believed about forgiveness – that life was stunted without it. Soon she must go the chapel for prayers, look at the image of the crucified Christ, and say, 'Forgive us our trespasses as we forgive…' It was simply the only way. To refuse forgiveness was to set a dam against the current of the river.

Remember the broken Christ, she told herself, and caught sight of the rosary beads hanging at his waist. Her rosary! Had he carried it all these years, like a child clinging to a blanket?

Jankin watched her face and did not trust himself to speak. The possibility that Thomasin might be alive filled his mouth and fought to be spoken, but he had caused Anna enough suffering without giving her false hope now. He must go to Winnerburn himself, see the young woman, and find out if she really were Thomasin of Hollylaw. It was hard to let Anna go on believing she was dead, but it would be harder to let her down.

If Thomasin had lived, it was to Falcon's credit, not his. He had ordered her death. He still needed to be forgiven.

'Can you even forgive me for Thomasin?' he said.

Forgive Jankin of High Crag Tower? She wasn't sure. She could forgive Brother John, who grieved over the past.

'Yes,' she said. 'Yes, I do.' And she felt completely, wonderfully free. The river could follow its course. A door had opened for her.

'Come with me,' she said. 'If you are to take medicines with you, you must know how to use them. If I could come with you to Winnerburn, I would.'

He left at first light the following morning with medicines and salves, food and drink, and a horse lent to him by Mother Gabriel. Need drove him on, the need to find the woman who might be Thomasin, and the need to keep quiet. If he stayed in Anna's presence much longer he might not have been able to resist telling her what he had heard. He must go, quickly.

It was strange to be riding a horse again, stranger still and uncomfortable to be riding while dressed as a monk. Given breeks, shirt and jerkin, boots and belt and a sword at his side, he could still have ridden these moors with a show and a swagger. As it was, by the time he felt at home in the saddle his hip was aching. Soon the pain was intolerable, and he walked instead, leading the horse. It was a fine horse, but unused to the steep, uneven rocks and moors. Sweat made the rough weave of the habit prickle his skin.

He would make the best speed he could to Winnerburn, but if summer diseases had already struck he would be too late for some. There would be deaths and heartbreak before he reached it. He had not allowed for a problem that made it all far worse.

It took only one chance meeting with a hill shepherd, but the news spread that a man with healing skills was on his way across the moors. Somewhere a child was dangerously sick, somewhere else a young mother was close to death. 'Brother, please, you must come.' By the end of the day he was hardly nearer to Winnerburnhead than when he had started, and he feared that he would have to return to AT– to Sister Penitentia for more medicines. He must travel as far as he could before night. His injuries pained him more and more, and when he dismounted and led the horse over steep hill paths and bogs, he found his breath was short. Old curses rose to mind and he tried not to mutter them. At a shepherd's hut he stopped, regained his breath, and was suddenly silenced.

The late twilight stunned him into reverence and brought him to his knees before his God. Darkness was coming in gently. Trees and moors stood against a clear violet sky laced with gold. He had laboured through this moorland all day, but it was only now that he looked at it, the rough bristling heather, the thronging bracken that made him cough, the harsh rocks, the winding silver streams and weaving swifts. It startled him to realize that he loved it. Every tussock and lichen, every blade of grass and stem of heather, he loved it; joyfully, warmly, honestly.

Chapter Fifteen

Thomasin no longer wore her necklace. She was a mother now, and Cal might hurt himself on the hard edges, or grasp at it and snap it. She had wrapped it up carefully and put it in the carved wooden box where Joan kept her few small treasures.

She disliked this unhealthy weather. It brought disease, headaches, bad tempers and bad memories. Creeping and flying things cheated their way into houses. But this morning she was woken by Cal's soft arms on her neck. That was the best sort of waking, the sweetest. To Cal she was not Tess. She was Mamam. She could surround him with her love as the sea enfolds an island. His warmth nestled into hers and she drifted into a sleep light enough to know that her son, morning-warm and drowsy, lay contented in her arms.

Loud, distressed voices were far away, but they forced her to pay attention. Joan was proclaiming about something – 'Poor little mite, poor mother!' Thomasin hugged Cal tightly and wriggled down below the blanket; then a door banged and Joan marched in. Slowly and with resentment, Thomasin sat up.

'Tess, Michael, will you lie here all morning?' said Joan. 'This isn't like you! Oh, here's Cal, God love him! Cal, come to your Nan and let Mamam and Dada get dressed. Michael, cover yourself up! Tess, I've just had Mistress Elliot here and there's a littlie died in the village, poor love. Jessie Hart's baby died, and the little lass is sick, and Ralph at the forge…'

Thomasin was wide awake, clutching Cal as Joan reached for him. 'Did you go near her?' she demanded.

'Why, of course I did!' exclaimed Joan.

Thomasin scrambled from the bed, still holding on to Cal. Joan stared at her.

'I didn't go touching anyone, if that's what you mean,' said Joan. 'And it's not Mistress Elliot who's been ill. Here, let me dress Cal.'

'I'll do it,' said Thomasin. 'I should have been up long ago.'

With Cal helping to carry the bucket, she fetched water from the spring. They brought lavender and bee balm into the house, where Cal gleefully tossed it among the rushes as she had taught him to. She put fennel seed and pennyroyal in the chest to keep fleas away. At midday she took bread and beer to the harvesters in the fields, insisting that Cal wore his hat against the strong sun.

'I tell you,' muttered Cuthbert, 'if I stood still she'd scrub me down with vinegar and hang flowers round my neck.'

'Be quiet and drink your beer,' ordered Joan. 'Holy Mother, who's that screaming?'

A young woman, helping with the harvest, had left her baby asleep under the shadow of a cart. When she went to feed him, surprised that he had not yet woken and cried, she had let out such a howl that scythes were dropped, sheaves were abandoned and every man, woman and child in the fields swarmed to her.

It was too late.

Thomasin stayed back, unwilling to intrude on grief and even more unwilling to take Cal into the wailing throng. It occurred to Joan that it was strange, the way they all seemed to look at Tess as she kept her distance. But it was a busy day, and she had soon forgotten that detail of it.

Another child fell ill the next day. Thomasin said at dinner time that she thought it must be the water making them sick, or maybe the insects. The wasps had been early this year. Last time she'd been on an errand to Alice Chisholm's there had been wasps buzzing round Philippa and Thomasin had flapped them away, but she couldn't be there all the time. All she could do was to remind Alice that vinegar was good for wasp stings. There were always so many rats at harvest time, too, and they were nasty, dirty creatures. Michael said he had heard that a holy man was about on the moors, and he might be able to help them.

An old man was suddenly taken ill. Philippa was stung by wasps. Alice sat up all night with her and became worn and nervous. The miller's wife miscarried.

Coming back from the fields one evening, Cuthbert held back. He needed to speak to his son.

'There's things being said about your Tess,' he said.

'So what if there are?' said Michael with a set face.

'Listen, son,' growled Cuthbert, 'I'm not saying anything against her. I don't think there *is* anything against her, except I can't get a seat in my own house once she gets in her fussy moods. But it's not her moods. It's *her*.'

'What about her?'

'Oh, wake up, Michael!' Cuthbert glanced over his shoulder and drew nearer to his son. 'There's more pestilence about than is normal, so they want someone to blame. Your Tess is a newcomer, and we know next to nothing about her. How clear do I have to make it, son? Are you being dim on purpose?'

'I'll not hear her spoken ill of!' Michael snapped back.

'Oh, you will,' said Cuthbert. 'That's exactly what I'm trying to tell you. She's unknown, she has skills that the other girls can't match, she has these moods. She won you, didn't she? There's a few lasses haven't forgiven her for that.'

'Are you saying…' began Michael.

'I'm saying nothing, son! I think she's a jewel of a lass, and that's why I'm warning you. It's other people are saying it, and you need to know.' He lowered his voice. 'They're talking of curses and the evil eye and such things I don't like to name. There's children and beasts sickening, but it's not touched our family, nor our beasts.'

'That's because we live out on the moor!' said Michael. 'And because Tess has been scouring the house all summer.'

'No good telling them that,' said Cuthbert. 'They'll believe what they want to believe. Heat and rumours and bad feelings – you'd be amazed what they can do. Suddenly, neighbours fight wars, and they're vicious, filthy wars. Strangers become evil, housewives become witches. Glances are curses, a wart is a devil's teat, a bonny bit of a necklace is a wicked charm, and so it goes. You want to get your Tess somewhere safe.'

'You can't spare us from the farm,' said Michael.

'I said her, not you. Maybe she could go to Jannie's for a while?'

'She'd have to come back, sooner or later,' said Michael, and fell silent, trying to think. Things like this should be sorted out properly by a local court, but it was too long to wait and too far to travel for that. The most powerful men in the valley were Sarah and Alice's husbands, and they wouldn't do any favours for Tess Wishart. A priest could sort it, but the priest was usually absent or drunk, or both.

'The holy man!' he said.

'The one that's about on the moor?'

'Aye. He's a real holy man from what I've heard, and he carries medicines and that. If I can find him, he might come and tell them to leave our Tess alone. He'll look after their sicknesses and tell them it's nothing to do with Tess. They might listen to him.' The more he thought of it, the more it seemed to be their best hope. 'I'll set out tonight.'

'Tonight? You'll not see an inch in front of you.'

'Morning, then. I'll go in the morning.' He wondered where Tess kept her necklace. His mother would know.

He left before dawn, kissing Thomasin very lightly so she would not wake. Then he saddled the horse and galloped away across the moor. Cuthbert invented a story – Jannie's husband needed help with the beasts, and Michael had ridden over at first light.

Then they came for Thomasin.

After days of travel and nights of hard sleeping, Jankin woke early and in pain, in the hollow of a rock. Mist had crept damply into his clothes, his bones, his throat and his burning chest. Breathing was painful, and his hip had stiffened so badly that even sitting up was a slow, grudging process, degree by degree. *I am alive*, he told himself, *alive with God in my heart and pain to carry for the world*. Something strong always seemed to remain in his heart, though his body groaned and his mind growled. He stamped and rubbed warmth into his limbs before kneeling to pray, then led the horse to a stream.

What happened here? As the mists lifted, the feeling grew upon Jankin that he knew this place, but not in a pleasant, familiar way. There was a darkness about it, as if he had woken from a dream into a nightmare. It was as if some spectre had come at him through the mist here, and he could not run.

The horse lifted its head, snorted and shook. Then it pricked its ears, turned and whinnied.

Hoof beats. Distant. Wait. Wait. Nearer. Coming this way.

A horseman was riding through the mists, and Jankin remembered. Years ago he had been the horseman, riding fast and hard to leave behind the screams of Hollylaw and High Crag Tower – but he had carried those screams in his head, and however furiously he rode he could not escape from himself. He had ridden this far. Here, on this rock, he had seen her waiting for him, the dead girl, her hair wet, her eyes wild with hate, her hands ready like claws to tear out his heart, crying out in vengeance for Anna's death.

He stood with one hand on the horse's flank, awaiting the horseman. He knew now that he had not seen Thomasin's ghost that day, but the memory had shaken him. With prayer in his heart, he waited. The horse tossed its head and stamped. He could see the rider now, and the young man must have heard the horse's whinny, for he turned sharply, rode down with a pounding of hooves, leapt from the saddle, and fell to his knees at Jankin's feet.

'Peace be with you,' said Jankin.

'Peace, brother,' said the man, quickly and carelessly as if he had no time for greetings. 'Sir, we need you, we need your help most desperately, sir, at Winnerburn. Will you come with me?'

'I am on my way to Winnerburn,' said Janking, putting out his right arm to help the tousle-haired young man to his feet. 'I heard that many of you are sick, and you need help.'

'It's worse than that, sir. It's my wife. She's in terrible danger, only you can save her, sir, and...'

'Tell me all, and tell it clearly,' said Jankin.

Standing up, Michael found himself a head taller than the

holy man, then realized that this was because the monk had a twisted leg and a crooked shoulder, and did not stand straight. His left arm seemed incapable of any movement at all, and he wheezed. Whatever potions he might have in that satchel, he couldn't cure himself. If this cripple was all they had to come between Winnerburn and disease, between Tess and her accusers, Michael had wasted time in seeking him. He should be home, putting all to rights himself, by whatever means he could, by boot and fist if nothing else could save her.

'I shouldn't trouble you, sir,' he muttered. 'Just, please, give me your blessing, and I'll go.'

He knelt again, waiting to receive the blessing as the priest raised his right hand, but that hand did not sign a blessing over him. It landed on his shoulder with a grip that dragged him to his feet, and the monk was barking into his face.

'You come riding down at me like a horseman from hell, and tell me you don't need me? Does your village suddenly not need healing, does your wife not need saving, though you've yet to tell me what she needs saving from? Or do you think that somewhere in this wet wilderness of sheep you can find a better helper? One who looks like a bishop and rides like a knight? Do you want to go looking for one?'

'I'm sorry, sir, please, I –'

'Tell me your name.'

'Michael Wi–'

'Michael will do. I am Brother John of High Crag Linn. Help me to my horse, Michael, and ride with me. Tell me your story as we go.'

Michael grabbed the bridle of Jankin's horse and held it steady while Jankin, still determined to do everything one-handed without help, heaved himself into the saddle. They rode side by side.

'Now, tell me,' he said, urging the horse to a trot.

Michael told him of the sicknesses in Winnerburn, which sounded to Jankin like the usual things, the sorts of things that Anna had taught him to... *Not Anna – Sister Penitentia, call her Sister Penitentia, remember that face – God forgive me, that was my wedding gift to her...* Michael was telling him something about his wife, who was accused of causing death by witchcraft...

'WHAT!'

Into Michael's story had fallen a word that struck like an arrow in the face. *Hollylaw.*

'I said she came from Hollylaw,' said Michael in surprise. 'When it was sacked by Hawk Jankin and his crew. She never talks of it. When she first came, she never said anything at all – she couldn't.'

'Tell me her name.'

'Tess,' said Michael, and glanced sideways at the monk. 'It's not her real name, it's what we call her.'

Jankin felt the rush of fear and excitement that used to come with a fight.

'What *is* her real name?'

Michael looked steadily ahead, between his horse's ears. 'I promised her not to tell it,' he said.

Jankin stopped so abruptly that Michael had to rein in his horse and turn. 'Then I know it,' he said. 'Did you say she's accused of witchcraft?'

'But she's no witch, Brother!' cried Michael. 'It's just because she's not from here, and they're jealous...' He urged the horse forward again. Jankin was riding ahead, quickening the pace.

'She has an ornament, the only one she has, a trinket, but it's better than anyone else has around us, and it's gey dear to her. I brought it with me, sir, so they wouldn't find it and take it away from her, nor break it, nor say it's a witch thing.' With the reins in one hand he reached into his jerkin for the twist of jewelled silver hanging from his shirt lacing. 'If it were up to me, I'd say, have it sir, and welcome, if you can save her!'

Jankin stopped. The necklace flashed in the sun. He saw Anna on her wedding day, and Thomasin, tear-stained and dirty, flying at him with that one beautiful thing around her 'neck.

'Where will they take her?' he demanded.

'The river, sir!'

'The river?'

'That's what they do, sir, they do it the old way. They'll tie her up and throw her in. If she sinks, the water has accepted her and she's innocent, but she's drowned. If she floats, she's guilty, so they'll put her to death.'

'Michael,' Jankin said. 'Point me the way to Winnerburn, and I swear I will ride as if every life I ever held dear depended on it. But you must ride with all your skill and strength to Hallowburn, to the Sisters of the Magnificat. Greet Mother Gabriel and ask, in my name, for Sister Penitentia. Do you have that name? Penitentia. Tell Sister Penitentia she must come with you at once, with no delay. Tell her about your wife, tell her you met me, tell her that Thomasin is alive!'

Michael's eyes widened. 'How did you...'

'GO!' rasped Jankin and, as Michael turned his horse away, he kicked his mount's flanks, rose in the saddle and rode with all the strength of his heart and soul to Winnerburnhead.

He had thought she was Anna's shadow. Then she had seemed to be his. But Anna was alive, Thomasin was alive. It was time to step out from the shadows.

Chapter Sixteen

'Come away from the window, Tess,' said Joan, but Thomasin was already sweeping Cal from the floor and pushing him into Joan's arms.

There had been rain in the night, leaving the river full and fast and the ground muddy underfoot. Thomasin heard the squelch of boots, coming nearer, getting louder. That was why she had rushed to the window and snatched up Cal to keep him safe, as she had kept him safe all his life. They had told her Michael had gone to find a priest or some such, but nobody knew when he would be back. Not soon enough.

What did they think they were doing, bringing foul airs and dirt up to Winnerburnhead? All summer she had struggled from first light to end of day to keep this house gleaming and ordered, to keep Cal safe from contagion, and now they would come crowding into the house with their filthy boots, their stinking breath, even their pitchforks and scythes!

'Don't let them in!' she whispered to Joan.

'We won't,' said Joan, but her face was troubled.

'We may not be able to stop them,' muttered Cuthbert.

Thomasin's fingers curled on her gown. 'But I've done nothing!'

'I'll sort them,' grunted Cuthbert. 'It's them in the town that get their way these days, but an old farmer from the hills still has a voice. Let's see what I can do.'

'Please don't let them in,' whispered Thomasin.

'She should have gone with Michael,' muttered Joan. 'We should have made her.'

'They would have taken that as a sign of guilt,' said Cuthbert. 'They would have found her.'

Thomasin shuddered violently, and felt cold. She had thought she was safe here. She did not want to be found.

'Joan, keep Cal safe,' she said. 'Whatever happens, don't let anyone harm Cal.'

'And we won't let them harm you, either,' said Joan firmly. She shifted Cal to her other hip as Cuthbert flung open the door so powerfully that it banged from the wall. He filled the doorway with his presence in a way that reminded Thomasin of Alan and Will at Hollylaw. Realizing that her knuckle was in her mouth, she whipped it out and stood tall with her hands folded in front of her. She must not look afraid, especially in front of Cal.

Here they were, big, rough, red-faced, sweaty men with bony hands, tall men with gawping mouths, women with fear and curiosity sharp on their faces. Alice was with them, her face drawn, blotched and ill, with her husband's friend the farrier holding her up. Little Philippa was clinging to her skirt.

'Neighbours, what's this?' called Cuthbert.

Watt Chisholm, Alice's husband, stepped forward. He was tall and better dressed than the others, with an air of authority in his strong, dark features.

'My wife has been plagued and troubled all night with cramps and nightmares,' he began.

'Then why isn't she home in bed?' demanded Joan, but Watt ignored her.

'As you know, she has miscarried a child this year,' he said.

'We believe that your Tess put the evil eye upon her and on our daughter.'

'No!' cried Thomasin. Watt stepped forward, but Cuthbert barred the door.

'You're there, are you, mistress witch?' he called. 'We want words with you!'

'Don't come in!' shrieked Thomasin. She stepped in front of Joan and Cal. 'I'll come out to you if you want me to!'

'You won't, Tess!' growled Cuthbert without turning his head. 'These gentlemen have started drinking early today. You have, Watt, I can smell it. There's a few heads need cooling down, that's all. Away you go, lads.'

Watt strode up to Cuthbert, standing much too close, insolently close, as if his sweat and bristle could touch Cuthbert's face as he spat out the words, very slowly and clearly.

'She'll come out,' he said, 'or we'll come in.'

Cuthbert stood still. Watt drew back his fist. Thomasin shrieked and sprang, knocking Cuthbert off balance, seizing Watt's arm and wrestling with both hands to draw it to her teeth. Then both of his arms were round her waist and the breath of his laughter stank past her.

'You wanted to come out,' he laughed grimly. 'You're out! Now we'll all go to the river. Best place to be, in the circumstances.'

'River?' gasped Thomasin. Behind her, Joan screamed, Cuthbert shouted and boots trampled over her clean floor. She thrashed and twisted to look over her shoulder – the tall men had to duck to get into the house, then there was an overpowering crash as the kitchen table was flung over. Above Joan's cries of anger and protest rose Thomasin's scream of fury.

'Get out of my house!' With all her strength she fought against the rough hands that held her fast. 'Out of my house! Joan, take Cal away! Out of…'

'Oh, it's your house, is it?' sneered someone.

Watt called over his shoulder. 'Search till you find her witch things – unless, Mistress Tess, you want to tell us where they are? Save Mistress Wishart from having her house searched?' Cuthbert was shouting in protest, but two men dragged him into a corner and held him there.

'I have no witch things!' cried Thomasin. Tossing her head as she struggled, she caught sight of Alice's drawn, pink face. There was no smile, but a look of smug triumph that urged Thomasin to slap her. She tried to gabble prayers in her head.

Please God, don't let them near Cal. Father, Son and Holy Spirit, don't let them near Cal. Angels of heaven, don't let them near Cal. Holy Mary, Mother of God, don't let them near Cal, have mercy. I'm sorry, I'm sorry for everything, don't let them near Cal. Anna, Anna in heaven, help us, don't let them near Cal… Cal was crying, and the sound tore at her heart as they dragged her from the house.

Joan turned Cal to the window to keep him from seeing the men who threw open the chest and kicked over the log basket. 'Let's see the sheep,' she said, though her voice was lost in his crying. 'Let's see if your Dada's coming.'

Thomasin tried to see who was there as they dragged her across the moor to the river. Would nobody in this place care what happened to her? Was the whole town against her? She recognized the huge, grey-haired form of Rob Foster, Sarah's husband. It was as if he had brought an army: all the relations, the workers and the friends of the Foster and Chisholm families, men who had shared beer and stories with Cuthbert every market day, women she had seen week by week with their children at their skirts, but they did not look like the Monday by Monday faces. The men reeked of drink. It wasn't as if they all had the same look about them; in some it was fear, in some it was hatred, in some it was suspicion or simple curiosity, in some it was the maddened look of a drunken man looking for a fight, but it all combined together to drown out all that was reasonable, sane and kind – all that was human. The voices muttered, rumbled and laughed; they rose, they cheered on Watt and Rob, like the baying of – no, not beasts. One single beast.

To Thomasin, looking through the tangle of hair in her eyes, the river looked wider and deeper than it had ever looked. It was as deep as bottomless hell, as wide as the way to destruction. It rushed its debris of twigs and leaves downstream as if nobody must steal its prey.

I survived High Crag Tower for this, thought Thomasin, staring in bewilderment at the faces round her. These people would call Falcon evil, but Falcon had spared her.

Falcon spared me. Something strong rose in her heart. Falcon had spared her, and because of that she had known years of being loved. Joan and Cuthbert had taken her into their home and into their hearts. Michael loved her, and she had Cal, and it would be a terrible thing for Cal to lose his mother – but Falcon had let her go, and she had been loved.

Watt heaved her round with her back to the river. Cuthbert had followed them and was shouting something, but nobody would listen.

'Let the girl answer the charges,' bellowed Watt. 'If she's innocent, she has nothing to fear.'

'There should be a priest!' yelled Cuthbert.

'No time to go looking for him and bring him here,' said Watt. 'And no use waiting for a court to try her, neither – she could have killed half the valley by then and cursed the harvest. Give us some space.'

Two of the men gripped Thomasin's arms. Watt and Rob stood a little to one side and in front of her, half turned towards her. A semicircle was forming. At her back, the river churned on.

'Tess Wishart of Winnerburnhead,' announced Watt. 'You caused Michael Wishart to became infatuated with you by witchcraft, and all your skill comes from the same witchcraft. You put your evil eye and your ill wishing on my wife, Alice Chisholm, causing her to miscarry, and on Philippa, to have such fits that she is withered for ever.'

'No!' cried Thomasin. 'Prove it!'

'My wife witnessed you threatening Philippa at our own home, only two weeks past.'

'I wouldn't do that!'

'Silence, witch!' he ordered. The man on Thomasin's left seized a handful of her hair and forced her head back.

'Shut your mouth!' growled Rob Foster.

'I saw her,' called Alice plaintively. 'She made magical passes over my little girl. Then she said that I'd need vinegar for wasp stings, and in no time after that I heard Philippa crying! She'd been stung, just like Tess threatened!'

'It wasn't –' began Thomasin.

'SILENCE!' roared Watt.

Inquisitive women sighed and shook their heads. They didn't want to believe it of Michael's Tess, but really, it was coming to look very much as if it was all true. Of course, if she really were a witch, she'd have had them all deceived, all this time.

Thomasin stood as tall as she could. She hadn't been dragged to High Crag Linn, tramped across moors and haunted by fear every day to be thrown into this great bullying river so the crowd could be entertained by whether she sank or swam.

'Let her speak!' shouted Cuthbert.

'Let her,' nodded Rob, as if he knew it would do her no good.

Thomasin raised her voice. 'There is no proof of witchcraft against me. I waved my hand at Philippa to keep the wasps away. Of course I warned Alice that she'd need the vinegar.'

'Your home,' said Watt, folding his arms, 'was always free from disease while all round the valley the folk and their beasts fell ill.'

'That's because we live a long way out,' she answered firmly.

'Do you live there so that you can practise your witchcraft with nobody knowing?' demanded Watt.

'I live there because that's where they took me in!' she cried.

'And there's other places far out where they've been ill,' said Watt. 'So how come your place is safe?'

'Because we keep everything so clean!' she insisted.

'Do you say the rest of us don't?' called a woman in the crowd. 'And what about Michael Wishart, who could have chosen any girl for miles about?'

Thomasin tilted her chin. 'I don't know,' she said. 'When he gets back, you can ask him.'

'Aye,' growled Rob. 'Where is he?'

'He's gone to find a man who'll judge me fairly!' she answered. She was proud of this, holding up her head and speaking for herself. If they wanted her to beg for mercy, they'd be disappointed.

'We should wait,' called Cuthbert. 'We have to wait until Michael brings him back.'

A glance passed between Alice and Watt. Thomasin saw Alice's lips move.

'And, while we wait,' continued Watt, 'if you've nothing to hide, Tess Wishart, why have you said nothing about where you come from and why you had to leave?'

The rushing of the river sounded louder and hungry. Thomasin struggled to speak against it.

'I come from Hollylaw,' she said. 'My home and everyone I had there, everything in my life, was destroyed when it was burned. I escaped over the moors.'

'We've only got your word for it,' said Watt. 'Nobody else from Hollylaw came here. Why would they, over that hill and the moors?'

A wince and a gasp from Alice made heads turn to see her swaying in the arms of the farrier. 'I'm not well,' she moaned.

Watt rounded on Thomasin. 'What are you doing, witch?'

'What's *she* doing?' cried Cuthbert. 'What do you think Alice is doing! Alice, you should be ashamed, after…'

Alice whimpered. Sarah ran from the crowd and whispered something to her husband.

'Witch signs?' he repeated. A murmur of excitement rode through the crowd like an echo of the river. They were closer.

'Where?' demanded Rob.

'On her arms,' said Sarah.

The men holding Thomasin pushed her arms forward. Their own grip had left weals of red and white across her skin amongst streaks of dirt. Rob bent over her to stare impudently at her upturned wrists.

'Sarah, show me,' he ordered.

Thomasin felt, rather than saw, the flicker of Sarah's eyes towards Alice. Then she stepped forward uncertainly and pointed with a shaking finger at the rough, scarred skin on

Thomasin's arms. The gashes she had given herself in High Crag Tower had healed unevenly, but nobody at Winnerburnhead had ever mentioned it.

Watt and Rob regarded each other like two doctors discussing a patient.

'Devil's marks,' said Watt.

'No doubt of it,' said Rob.

'What do you know about it?' Thomasin snapped back, and shrieked as Watt grabbed her by the shoulders.

'So *you* know about it, then?'

The crowd was pressing nearer, stretching and leaning sideways, all keen to see the witchmarks. The farrier's wife was supporting Alice in her arms.

'I got those scars escaping from Hollylaw,' insisted Thomasin.

'For God's sake, swim her!' cried the farrier's wife. 'Can't you see she's making Alice ill?'

'Can't you see Alice is play-acting!' cried Cuthbert, but nobody was listening.

Thomasin looked up. From the hills, she could see the young men who worked for Cuthbert and Michael running down the hills towards them, and her heart lifted. She was wondering if there was anything they could do when the cry of 'Swim her!' was taken up, growing louder, faster, like the beat of a drum: 'Swim her! Swim her!'

Cuthbert was forcing his way through the crowd. 'Please, just wait for Michael and the holy brother! You can't do this! At least, listen to me, the water should be blessed, and you can't do that without…'

'It's been blessed before, it doesn't wear off,' grunted Rob.

'What's this?' said Watt suddenly.

He was looking over the heads of the crowd. A tall young

man, one of the lads who had thrown themselves into the search of Joan and Cuthbert's house, was loping down the hill towards them in huge strides. Sweat and a huge gash of a grin glowed on his face.

'Found it!' he yelled.

Found what? Thomasin strained to see what he carried. Would it be her necklace, and who could possibly claim anything about that? But when she saw the glint of silver, hope left her.

She had been keeping that in case Jankin returned. Now, she wished she could ram it into that stupid grinning mouth.

In the farmhouse at Winnerburnhead, Joan took the largest log from the basket and gave Cal a rope to use for reins. That would be his horse. She chatted, and tried to keep busy, fighting tears and being strong for Cal.

'Where Mamam?'

'She had to go with the men, pet lamb.'

'Bad men.'

'Hush now, hinny.'

It looked very much as if she'd have to bring up Cal herself now. If they decided to tie up Thomasin and swim her, there was no hope but for a miracle. What would she tell Cal one day, when he wanted to know what had happened to his mother? Where was Michael?

Even Joan didn't know what they had found. She only knew that Michael and Tess's bed was sprawled all over the floor, and they'd gone climbing on each other's shoulders to scrabble about in the niche on the wall. She had no idea what was in there. Well, didn't all women have their little secrets, and for very good reasons, too? Did that make them witches?

Another furious banging on the door made her stomach

sicken and tears rise in her eyes. *For the love of the Saviour, haven't they done enough?* She picked up the poker and opened the door just enough to see, bracing herself with one hand against the door post. If anyone came near that child, they'd see what his grandmother could do.

She did not recognize the man who stood leaning his shoulder on the door frame as if his arm would not hold him up, struggling for breath. He wore a monk's robe, and gasped out the words, 'Where's Tho… Tess? Michael sent me.'

'They've taken her! Cal, come to Nan!'

'Where?'

'I'll show you, sir!'

The silver vial was passed from one to another, sniffed and handed on. Silently, Thomasin cursed them and herself. *If only I had destroyed it. Why didn't I? If only I'd left well alone, if only I hadn't climbed that chimney, if only…*

For Cal's sake, she must stay alive. She must find a way out of this.

'Tell us what it is,' ordered Watt. 'Is it a charm?'

'It's a keepsake that my old mistress gave me,' said Thomasin, trying to think two steps ahead – *what will they ask me next, what will I say…?*

'Strange keepsake,' commented Rob, sniffing the bottle again. 'It's got a sharp edge. Could be some witch thing.'

'I am not a witch!' she cried.

'If it's not a charm,' said Watt, 'it's a poison.'

'No!' shouted Thomasin. 'Why would I have poison?'

She heard the crowd soften into an ugly murmuring, and knew that she had made a mistake. *Why should she have poison?* She should have admitted that it was poison, and that she had kept it in case she needed to defend herself – but it was no good changing her story now. *If only*.

'Yes,' said Rob, 'we'd all like to know that. Why would you have poison? Who do you want to poison?'

'I'm not a poisoner!' cried Thomasin. 'I've never harmed anyone! Please!'

Cuthbert, shouting something, finally made his voice heard. 'It'll just be a medicine or something! Isn't that right, Tess?'

Dared she say it was a medicine? They might try it out on someone, even on her.

'I don't know what it is,' she pleaded. 'My mistress gave it to me, to look after it. I don't know what's in it.' *Angels, Mother of God, help me*.

'You don't know what it is,' said Watt, 'but you kept it hidden all these years.'

'It's from her old mistress,' shouted Cuthbert. 'Of course it's a medicine for something. Why would her mistress give her poison?'

She wished she could tell him. It was terrible to deceive Cuthbert but she bristled with hatred for Watt and Rob, who had taken control of her life and death. What business was it of theirs?

'Still,' went on Watt, 'if you're sure it's safe, try it. We'll find out.'

The crowd grumbled. He turned to them, planting his feet apart, holding the vial high above his head.

'If she's innocent,' he said, 'God will protect her.'

The crowd grew louder, some urging him on, some no longer sure about it and murmuring protests. Cuthbert was shouting but his voice was growing distant, as if someone were dragging him away. Watt was forcing the bottle in front of Thomasin's face; she folded her lips tightly. Somewhere she could hear hooves, and the crowd was scattering. Watt was forcing the vial towards her as she turned her head away, but she had no choice – *Christ have mercy, I love you Cal, I love you, Michael, Christ receive me…*

It was too late to realize, as she did now, that she would give up all hope of vengeance and all her hatred of Jankin if she could only hold her son in her arms once more. A strong hand on the back of her head forced her face to the bottle. The bitter tang was too close as she squeezed her eyes shut. *Cal, my beautiful son…*

There was a blow, a shout and a clang of metal on stone. She opened her eyes and looked down to see a thin liquid soaking into the ground. A sandal kicked the vial into the river with a whirl of silver.

'In God's name,' cried a man's voice, 'let her go!'

Chapter Seventeen

The men did not let go altogether, but their hold on her arms and shoulders slackened so suddenly that her legs buckled. Nausea and dizziness left her at the top of High Crag Linn – no, before that, in the tower, when she had tried to kill Jankin; the past was swirling over her like filth in a pool.

Somebody was speaking. There was a man with a voice that carried authority, even though it gasped for breath and carried an old man's wheezing in a younger man's voice. Rob and Watt were demanding to know who this stranger was.

'Peace,' said the voice. It was gentle and less breathless now, but the word was followed by a painful cough. 'I am Brother John of High Crag Linn, and in the name of Christ, in the love of Christ, I ask you to release her and let me deal with this case.'

She craned her neck to see him, but Watt, Rob and the others stood in front of her. Leaning to see through the gaps between them she could see only a crooked figure in a plain, rough habit. A rosary hung from his waist. There was something familiar about that rosary. Rob and Watt, and Alice, who seemed to have regained her strength, were earnestly telling him all she was accused of. Cuthbert was desperately getting in a phrase when he could.

'Peace,' said the hermit again. There must have been some air of authority in his look, too, because even Watt fell silent while Cuthbert spoke up for her and Thomasin tried to see better. Then the monk seemed to take over.

'I know her story,' he said gravely. 'I know it far better than any of you do. It may be that she carried poison, but there was a time when she might well have needed it.'

They were parting to let him through. She saw the crookedness of his gait and the way one arm hung unmoving, with one shoulder higher than the other. She saw the straggly hair, the lean face marked with lines of suffering, and the deep, brave eyes which could not be the eyes of Hawk Jankin, but were.

God have mercy. I always knew he would come back, Hell fiend! He couldn't just die, he couldn't settle for murdering Anna and all of Hollylaw, he had to come back for me. Old hatred fought its way to the surface. Now she could denounce him, spring at him as she had before and claw his face – but it was as if her feet had grown into the earth.

He stepped forward, looking into her eyes, and she shrank back. She opened her mouth to scream, but could not.

'She flinches from the holy monk!' said Rob, but Jankin ignored him.

'If I could have saved your life by drinking it,' he said quietly, 'I would.'

'Look at her eyes!' snarled Watt. 'She's terrified of him! If that's not a sign that she belongs to the devil, what is?'

'She's struck dumb!' said Rob.

'She was dumb when she came here,' wailed Alice. 'Just as if the devil had locked up her tongue.'

'And what price did she pay him to get it back?' demanded Rob, but Jankin's cry of 'Silence!' rose above him. Jankin turned his back on Thomasin.

That was better. She could breathe more easily. She did not

have to look into his face, and he had placed himself between her and her accusers.

'Come to your senses!' shouted Jankin. 'This woman has suffered terrible wrongs, and you are heaping more upon her! I know her story, I know her to be be brave and true. If you knew of her courage and loyalty, you would gasp at it. You should come before her now and beg her forgiveness. As should I.'

He turned and knelt at her feet.

Thomasin stood still as a boundary stone. Hate was a habit that would not easily break. Now was the time to kick the humped shoulder and the lame leg, call him murderer, hellhound, imposter, deceiver, and how dare he turn up wearing that habit as if he'd had a rosary, not a sword, at his side when he rode down to Hollylaw? The memory of it made anger crackle in her heart and tingle in her hands.

But here he was, pleading for her life, kneeling at her feet, asking her forgiveness, standing between her and her accusers, calling her brave and true. If not for him, her own poison would be twisting through her guts at this second. Because of him, she might see Cal again.

'You…' she began, but the words would not come.

The crowd, not knowing whom or what to believe, drew back and whispered to each other. What was she trying to say?

'She tries to curse the holy brother,' announced Watt. 'You all heard it. Rob, do you have the rope?'

Thomasin shrieked. She had not noticed the rope.

Joan had done what she needed to do – she had directed Brother John to the river and, though she could not keep pace with his horse, followed to make sure he found the place. She had left Cal in the care of a girl who had come in to do the laundry, but the girl found it difficult to watch Cal and do the washing at the same time, and didn't want to risk him being scalded or hurt. She had tethered him with a long rope to the roof post, and not noticed that he was quietly wriggling the knot over his head. By the time she realized that it was strangely quiet, he was running eagerly on strong little legs to the river.

'Leave this to us, brother,' ordered Watt. 'We're the ones she offended, and we'll deal with this. The water is a blessed element, we know what we're doing.'

'It hasn't been blessed!' cried Cuthbert.

'It's good enough,' said Rob. 'If it accepts her, she's innocent. If she floats, she's guilty, and then she might even live long enough for that court you keep talking about.'

'But if she drowns, you will have killed an innocent!' Joan was elbowing her way through the crowd, crying out, pushing the gawping men aside. 'What if she's with child again? You'd kill an innocent babe! Tess, are you…'

At the sound of Joan's voice Thomasin stretched up, straining to look over the crowd. 'Joan!' she shouted. 'Where's Cal?'

Joan was shouting back, but suddenly the noise of the crowd rose and she could hear nothing. The rope was uncoiled and her feet were kicked from under her. This was not happening in a far off tower, but here, where she had found a home, in the bright light of a sunny day. Chaos and bloodlust still churned through the crowd. There was a mood for a fight and a drowning, breaking through into a moment when all the rules of behaviour, peace and neighbourliness could be torn apart or discarded, and no strange monk would spoil it. Some of them were holding Jankin, Cuthbert and anyone else who tried to defend Thomasin, dragging them back so that scuffles were breaking out between the Wisharts' supporters and the Chisholms'. A gag was forced round her mouth, her head was pushed down, and with a wrench they were forcing her arms to cross, tying hand to foot and foot to hand. The most terrible part of it all was her helplessness. Trussed and carried, she could do nothing to help herself, and it would have been better to hurtle down High Crag Linn and be broken, with nobody to watch, than to be bundled up and drowned slowly to satisfy the wild beast. She couldn't even say the words that needed to be said – a prayer, a farewell, anything – but she screamed through the gag as mauling hands grabbed at her, lifted her and swung her so that her gown flapped and their jeers rose all around her. There were shouts of protest from Joan, Cuthbert, Jankin, her friends and, though the gag silenced her, everything inside her screamed as they swung her like a flour sack through the air.

ONE!

Lord, have mercy! Anna! Joan, Cuthbert, tell Cal I love him! I will always love him! Michael, Michael!

TWO!

Lord, have mercy, Anna, help me, Mother of God, help me, Christ have mercy! Oh, dear God, rescue me, saints and angels, help me!

THREE!

In the seconds before she sank, she thought she heard Cal cry for Mamam.

The shock of cold water tumbled her over, chilled through her clothes, beat in her ears, dragged and drenched and flung her. It filled her gown and lifted her so that she gulped fresh air before it somersaulted her down again and roared in her ears so that the screaming crowd vanished. Thrashing, writing, she fought for the surface and for air.

'Enough!' yelled Cuthbert from the crowd. The mood was changing now. It had gone far enough.

'We never meant to harm her, it was just to teach her a lesson, put her in her place, not this, it got out of hand…'

Cuthbert's lads and the older men and women were moving in, running along the bank to help her, forcing aside the men who held Joan and Cuthbert. Thomasin's dark head disappeared beneath the water and bobbed up again further downstream – for a second her face appeared as she gulped a lungful of air.

Two or three young lads hauled Watt away from Jankin and a blow from Jankin's one good arm felled Rob. More of them were flying along the bank.

The river carried Thomasin on. It would be deeper soon, and the current stronger. It flung her against the bank, where she scrabbled with her tied fingers to grip a tree root, but it was too wet, too slippery; she tried again, as cramp gripped her leg.

'Throw the rope!' shouted someone on the bank.

'She can't hold it!' yelled Jankin and ran along the riverbank, overtaken by younger and stronger men as they pulled off their jerkins, leapt into the water, and splashed their way to her. He sprawled on the bank, reaching out. All around Thomasin, the rough, brown arms of farmworkers reached towards her.

Thomasin tried to see through the water in her eyes. Somebody had caught her! They were pulling and heaving her to the bank. Dry arms stretched to her, Jankin was helping to haul her up, and she was out, with the dry earth beneath her. There was the rasp of a knife, and her crying, cramping limbs were free.

'All over now, Thomasin,' whispered a hoarse voice in her ear. Cal had run off in search of Mamam and his grandmother.

He had called for Mamam and could not see her, but he could hear a lot of shouting and splashing from near the river. He liked the river. The grown-ups would never let him get as close to it as he wanted, and he only wanted to lean over it, to see if there were any fishes. This time, there were no grown-ups to stop him. He could get as close as he like, to look for the fishes. There weren't any today. But there was a stone, right at the edge of the water, shining wet and just the right size to climb on.

Shuddering took every cell of Thomasin. Her teeth chattered. Water streamed from her hair and her clothes, blurring her eyes and shouting in her ears. Somebody pressed a jerkin round her. She coughed up water.

Jankin, rubbing warmth into her arms, looked back along the stream. 'What's that?' he said.

A small brown bundle was hurtling down the river, tossed by the water like a plaything. A wet head emerged, the eyes closed and the mouth stretched in a cry.

'Cal!' screamed Thomasin and ran. Four, five, six of the men were running along the bank with ropes, belts and branches. Jankin dropped into the river.

Thomasin's wet skirts dragged at her, her feet could hardly feel the ground. She stumbled on, forgetting cold and soaked clothes, her eyes on the little head bobbing on the water, still screaming out his name; her world, her helpless little world, swirled further and further away from her in that deep dark water. Nothing else mattered, only Cal, Cal, Cal, and Jankin thrashing through the water towards him.

Jankin fought for breath against the tightness in his chest and the bruising pain of his breathing as he clutched at air, at water and finally at Cal's hand. A rope splashed on to the surface, just out of reach – if he could just get it – if he could fasten it one-handed around Cal… The water closed over his head. Cal was clinging to him with such terror that he was dragging them both down, and Jankin felt the current swallow him.

With all he had left of his old skill and strength he hoisted Cal above the surface. The withered arm could at least be a shelf to hold the lad up. Then strong hands lifted young Cal, and reached in again for Jankin, pulling him to the bank where Thomasin staggered forward, holding out shivering, goose-fleshed arms.

Shaking and frightened, Cal and Thomasin clutched each other against the cold and the world's cruelty. When Thomasin looked over Cal's head to see the men kneeling by the bank, dragging Jankin from the water, she stretched down a hand to help them haul him to land.

Suddenly everybody was rushing to help, taking off shirts and jerkins to wrap around them, trying to dry her hair, rubbing her hands, offering to fetch dry clothes. It was as if they had woken from an evil enchantment and were desperate to prove that they were on her side, that they cared, that none of them had ever believed her guilty. Still kneeling on the bank, she allowed Joan to take Cal from her, peel off his wet clothes and wrap him in somebody's dry shirt, but she pushed away the cloak that someone offered her.

'He needs it,' she said, trying to rub warmth into Jankin's chilled shoulders. His eyes were closed. Water coughed from his mouth.

'Come away now, my hinny,' said Joan, pulling her to her feet. 'There's plenty of them here to look after him. Come away home, you and Cal, and we'll get you warmed up and dry before you catch something.'

Thomasin lingered. There was a blue tinge to Jankin's

skin, and with her ears still full of water she could not tell whether she heard him breathing.

'Get the holy man to our house,' ordered Joan. 'We'll look after him there. You lads, will you carry him to Winnerburnhead?'

There were a few crestfallen faces amongst the housewives who would have loved the privilege of caring for the holy man. Nobody who looked after the monk could be accused of being on the Chisholms' side in this bad business. But on this day nobody would argue with Mistress Wishart, and the men set about making a stretcher from jackets and branches.

'Is he still alive?' asked one.

'God knows,' said another.

Chapter Eighteen

In the guest house of the nunnery, Michael scuffed his boots and scowled. This should be a beautiful place. The garden was a joyful dance of colours, sweet and scented and singing with bees, the honey-gold stone was pleasantly cool, the room was airy – it was exactly what it should be, a house of beauty and peace. But it was no place for him, prowling and fuming as he turned his hat in his hand, waiting for the nun he had asked to see. They had questioned him as if he were a criminal – why did he want to see Sister Penitentia? Who was the man who had sent him? The sisters were at prayer; would he like refreshment and stabling for his horse? No, thank you, he would not.

He was not a monk, a hermit or a priest. A man alone – Mother Gabriel would have to be consulted. Finally, a novice led him to a plain chamber where a calm, middle-aged nun with an air of wise solemnity was seated behind a table. Another sister, heavily veiled, stood behind her.

'I am Mother Gabriel, the abbess of this house,' said the nun. 'Tell me your errand.'

He told it as quickly as he could. When he came to telling his wife's real name, there was such a cry from the veiled nun that he thought she must be in pain.

'Be seated, sister,' said Mother Gabriel quietly, and the nun glided to the window seat. 'Tell me a little more about your wife, Michael. Is she tall or short? Plump, thin? Dark, fair, red-haired?' The other nun made no more sound, but he could still feel her intense gaze, dragging at him, like Cal demanding his attention. When he placed the necklace on the table, she leaned forward to see.

'Thank you, Michael,' said Mother Gabriel. 'Please wait outside.'

Did these sisters have no sense of time? 'Madam,' he said, 'My cause is most urgent.'

'Wait outside, please,' she repeated. There was no point in arguing. He cast one pleading glance towards the other nun, hoping that she could see it behind all that veiling and could hurry things along, and left the chamber.

Anna lifted the veil, drying her eyes on it, and Mother Gabriel placed the necklace in her hands. It blurred and trembled, and Anna found she was stammering. It was all too much to take in.

'She's alive,' she whispered. 'And she's in danger again. I must go to her, Mother.'

'Sister Penitentia,' said Mother Gabriel, 'you have taken final vows and are a sister of this order. You are asking my permission to leave, suddenly, in the company of a man – a man of the world, not a priest, not a holy brother – to visit somebody who is part of your past life, and not a member of your family.'

'She *is* family,' said Anna, but Mother Gabriel ignored her and said nothing for a while, gazing from the tiny window as if she saw nothing. Then she turned back to Anna, who was stroking the silver necklace.

'There is disease in Winnerburn,' said Mother Gabriel softly, as if she were thinking aloud. 'That, of course, is why the brother from High Crag Linn first came here.'

'Then order me to go as a healer!' cried Anna.

'It is not within the rules of our order,' said Mother Gabriel, and looked out of the window again.

'Then if you won't order me, permit me to go,' said Anna. She put down the necklace and knelt. 'Mother Abbess, please, please, give me leave to go to the help of the people of Winnerburn.'

'You know perfectly well that you are concerned about only one of the people of Winnerburn,' said Mother Gabriel. 'But she is in danger of her life, and you may be able to help her as nobody else could.'

'Then please, Mother, let me go!' cried Anna.

With a sudden swish of her habit and a clink of rosary beads Mother Gabriel swept across the floor to look down at Anna.

'Sister Penitentia,' she said, 'I should not allow you to leave this house at all without an excellent reason, one that our superiors would understand.' She paused, and sighed. 'And I shall have to think of one, but in the meantime, go. Take what you need, heal the sick, and do what you can to help the woman known as Tess Wishart. Michael Wishart has a horse and you will need another – take the bay. I should send a sister as an escort, but Brother John has our only other riding horse. If word of this reaches the bishop I may have to dismiss you from the order or put you in a bare cell on dry bread and water, but go.' She raised her hand. 'And the blessing of God the Father, the Son and the Holy Spirit be with you on your journey and bring you safely back to us.'

She extended her hand. Anna kissed the ring, got to her feet and ran for the door, covering her face as she went.

The sun over Winnerburn set in streaks like the breath of angry angels. Watt Chisholm and Rob Foster, with their friends and family, slouched silently home. It had been the weather, the touch of evil in the heat, a midsummer madness making them behave the way they had. Alice, her face pink, hair straying from under her cap, scowled sullenly up at her husband. Trust a man to go about this in all the wrong way. Philippa would be fretful by the time she got home.

Men and women glanced uneasily from one to another, avoiding each other's eyes. They'd been right, of course, to be concerned about whether Tess were a witch. After all, she might have been, might she not. They had reason to suspect, and they had to protect our children. Rob and Watt had gone the wrong way about it. Just as well the holy man had turned up the way he did.

There was a secret understanding between Rob and Watt, though hardly a glance was exchanged. *I will forget that you shouted for them to swim her. You will forget that I laid hands on Cuthbert Wishart. I did not see you hold her down while they tied the knots. You did not hear me blame her for the death of Jessie Hart's baby. It all got out of hand, that's all. Our own part in it will seem much less in a day or two. It was a mistake, that's all. A few moments of bad judgment.*

A bed was made up for Jankin in the main room of Joan and Cuthbert's house, because that was the room with the fireplace in it.

'He's more dead than alive,' observed Joan. 'But he may as well die comfortable. I just wish he could tell me where Michael is.'

Jankin forced his eyes to open. The tearing pain in his chest had dulled to a steady throb, piercing his throat as he took a breath to speak.

'He went...' he must limit the words, for each one cost him dearly. 'Find... An... An... Ann... a...'

'Another brother?' wondered Joan, as Jankin's eyelids closed again. 'An… another helper, maybe?'

'Let him be,' said Cuthbert. 'How's our Tess? Shouldn't she be by the fire?'

'I sent her to her bed,' whispered Joan. 'But I doubt she'll sleep.'

Cal woke and whimpered. Thomasin rolled over on the bed to lift and rock him, pressing his warm pink cheek against hers, singing very quietly until the steady rocking started to make her own eyes heavy and she saw again the rushing water, and felt its anger, gushing over her head. When Joan came in with a warm posset, she was shaking again.

'Dear God and his angels, girl, what was I thinking about?' Joan sat down on the bed and folded an arm round her. 'Cuthbert's right, you should be by the fire too. Bring Cal, if you still won't let him out of your sight. Here, can I take him for a minute?'

With Cal tightly in her arms, Thomasin let Joan steer her to the fireplace. There, by handing her the posset, Joan was able to take Cal from her.

'Leave him where I can see him,' Thomasin said, so Joan sat him on a log again, one that would rock if he rode on it. Thomasin, feeling the need for human warmth, pressed up against Joan.

'Why have you always been kind to me?' she asked.

'Oh, Tess, my hinny, what a thing to ask!' said Joan.

Thomasin watched the flames flare and dance, and listened to them crackle. 'My name is Thomasin,' she whispered. It was a relief to say it. At the name, Jankin's eyelids flickered.

'Anna,' he croaked.

So he still thinks of her, thought Thomasin. *Or he's rambling.*

No point in asking about Michael, then.

Jankin's eyes opened and closed again. He tried to speak, but only coughed so violently that he lurched and fought for breath. Joan stroked his hair and straightened the blankets.

'Now, never you mind,' she said. 'You just be peaceful.' She took a cup from the hearth, and from the waft of thyme and bay Thomasin recognized the last of the mixture they had made for winter chills. She watched as Joan laid Jankin's head back on the pillow. His face was grey as a corpse.

This was still the man who had harried and bullied and destroyed Hollylaw.

He had burned her home and her friends.

He had killed Anna.

He had tried to kill her.

He had saved her.

He had killed Anna. And that was Anna's rosary in his hands, like a sign of repentance.

He had saved Cal.

He must have known it could kill him, but he had saved Cal.

He had broken her poison.

She felt free, and she had forgotten what that was like. It was as if the walls of High Crag Tower had collapsed around her, and she could walk into sunlight.

Hate, resentment, fear and the hope of revenge had held her up, but only in the way that the victim is held up by the stake. It wasn't even as if she wanted to transfer her hate to Alice and Watt, or any of them, because hate had gnawed her for long enough. She was free to love Michael, Joan and Cuthbert more than ever – even to love Cal more, if that were possible. Jankin had broken her poison, and there was no point in looking for more.

She and Joan took turns to watch with him that night. When she became sleepy, she found her spindle and fleece, and turned it steadily through the night. Once, he woke, and tried to speak, and she heard something about 'sorry' and 'Anna'. She hushed him. He had changed. Everything had changed and it would be a wonderful thing to change the past too. But not even she could spin backwards, and turn the thread back into fleece.

At sunrise, Joan came to take over. 'Praise God, you look better than you did!' she said, and fussed over Jankin, feeling his forehead and raising him so she could smooth the rough blanket beneath him.

Visitors arrived that day to enquire after Brother John, leaving soups, possets and honey. They were awkward and shy with Thomasin, and unusually respectful to Cuthbert and Joan.

'They'll settle down,' said Cuthbert. 'It'll all get to be the way it should, but it's no good trying to rush things. We go on with the harvest, same as we should. Wish I knew where our Michael had got to, but he's a big strong lad, he can look after himself. Off to find more help than one poor lame monk, I should think. The new Lord of Hollylaw, maybe.'

'Wherever he is,' said Joan, 'I'll not settle until he's home.'

Thomasin would have liked to ask Jankin about Michael, but he slept much, and could hardly speak when he woke. The next night, his breathing was worse.

'His lungs must be in a poor state,' remarked Joan. 'Probably have been for years. 'He's been in the wars, poor soul. What does a monk get up to, to bring him to that state?'

Thomasin had wondered that, too, holding the lamp to his face in the night, astonished that his face had aged so badly in only five years. She wondered what had happened to leave

202

him with that crippled leg and shattered shoulder, and his left arm useless. Maybe he really had fallen down the Linn.

He became more conscious, but could not speak. One morning, when Thomasin took her place beside him with a bowl of porridge to spoon into his mouth, he shook his head and struggled to talk.

'My... my...'

She tried to think it out. My what? He owned little enough.

'Your satchel is safe, with the medicines in it.'

He shook his head.

'Your horse?'

He scowled. 'My...'

'Oh!' she said. 'Michael!'

He nodded, slowly, and slowly reached his right arm across to grip her hand. 'He went... fetch... a...' even those few words were a struggle, and he could say no more. Thomasin frowned as she tried to think it through.

'A priest?' He shook his head. 'A man of law?' She saw the frustration on his face.

'An... An...'

An... An...

The little syllable, the first sound she had made when she came here, sang Anna's name into her head. But it couldn't be. She looked into his eyes. She must be horribly mistaken, so ridiculously, stupidly mistaken that she could only whisper.

'You mean, "Anna"?'

He tried to smile, but it was too hard.

Joan put bread into baskets and covered them with a clean cloth. She really would prefer to stay home today, as the poor man needed looking after, and she didn't like to leave him in anyone else's care, even with Tess – Thomasin – oh, she was so used to calling her Tess now. Tess could take the bread to the men in the fields at midday, and could help with the harvesting. She could just about spare Tess from the house today.

'Joan!'

She jumped. Tess, her gown flying, her eyes wild with joy, flew into the pantry and hugged her.

'I have to go, Joan, will you mind Cal this morning? I won't be long.'

Joan gawped with astonishment. 'Where? For how long? What are you doing?'

'I just have to go and see if they're coming…'

'If who's coming?'

'If… if Michael's coming, of course! I'll be back soon, I can't leave Cal for long.'

'Ask our Michael where he thinks he's been all this time!' Joan called, and watched as Thomasin ran out into the early sunlight, splashed through the stream, and scrambled up the hill at the other side. She shook her head. She had seen many things in her daughter-in-law's eyes before – fear, suspicion, hate and finally love, the mother-cat protective love she wove around Cal. But the wild hope that sent her flying from the house with her gown flapping and her hair undone was an unbearable joy, new and utterly unlike her. Was she with child again? She couldn't be, or she would have said so when they tried to drown her. Or was she suddenly as much in love with Michael as he was with her? About time. She picked up the spindle from the hearth. The girl who had twirled and twirled this spindle was behaving like a real ordinary lassie at last.

And here was Brother John, trying to sit up. With a strong arm, she raised him. It would be a fine thing when Brother John got his voice back. He must have some stories to tell.

Chapter Nineteen

Alice touched her face and looked at her reflection in the bowl of water. The bruises were almost gone. She could go out now. If the holy man was getting better, he might be able to help Philippa. It would be best to wait until everyone was out in the fields. Tess might be there. It would be just like Tess to be hanging around where she wasn't wanted. But at least she could walk up to Winnerburnhead with a gift for the holy man, and see if anyone was about.

Thomasin ran until her legs were too slow to run any longer, then she strode briskly, bracken and bilberry snagging on her skirt and with the sun in her eyes. The moors were so uneven that it was hard to see what was over the next ridge, or among the trees to the west; she should turn back soon, but the urge was to go on, a little further, to see if there was any sign beyond the stones, over the hill…

She should go back. If Anna were alive, and Michael had gone to find her, she could be at the other end of the country. It could be weeks before they got here. But she would climb one more hill for a last, good look, though the heat reddened and prickled her. On the hill top she sat down on a rock and pulled up a fern to fan herself.

Something was moving, far off. She watched.

Two horses. Two riders. They were still too far off to tell

who they were. She waited. They were nearer now, she knew Michael from the way he rode. She ran as if a fiery chariot had caught her up and swept her along.

Nobody answered Alice's tap at the door. She pushed it open, peeped round, and saw the holy man, his chin stubbly, sleeping in the bed they had made up by the fire. She had brought a cheese, and left it in the cool larder, then took Philippa on her lap and sat down to wait until he woke.

He did not wake. His breathing rattled and sometimes he coughed in his sleep, but he did not wake. She couldn't stay all morning. She'd be missed, and Watt would have something to say. She brushed away a tear. It wasn't fair that Tess should have the holy man to herself, as well as everything else that had fallen her way. Philippa was getting restless.

Brother John's eyelids were flickering. Alice darted to his side and laid a hand on his shoulder. His eyes opened fully.

'Please,' she said. 'Can you help my daughter? Can you make her well?'

The words were such a whisper that Alice had to bow her head to his lips to hear.

'She... is... well. Beautiful.'

He didn't seem to understand. She held up Philippa, so he would see the angled head and useless arm, and know what she was asking. He raised a hand. Slowly, clearly, he made the sign of the cross in blessing before drifting into sleep again.

Thomasin kept running and now the grey-robed nun dismounted and ran too, lifting the hem of her habit, stumbling over stones and clumps of grass. Thomasin would have called her name, but she couldn't spare the breath – then they were wrapped in each other's arms, too tightly hugged together to notice faces. *It's you! It's you!*

Alice stood up and took Philippa by the hand. They should go. It seemed to her that the room was getting cooler, and the sick man needed to be kept warm. She prodded the fire with the poker, and put on another log before she left.

Thomasin and Anna stepped apart at last, and held each other at arm's length. Thomasin put out her hand to the veil.

'I'm very ugly now,' said Anna, but did not stop her. 'I was burned.'

For the first time, Thomasin heard the awkward slur in Anna's speech. She lifted back the veil and winced a little when she saw the scarring, and thought of the pain that had caused it and the beauty that had been. In all her memories, Anna was beautiful. But Anna looked out at her from the wreck, and Anna's rough hand was in hers. Thomasin kissed the scars and looked past Anna to see Michael, smiling, patiently holding the bridles. He had waited, holding back from a moment that was nothing to do with him. He looked kind and pleased and, at the same time, a little lost, and Thomasin's heart reached out to him.

'Where's Cal?' he asked.

'With your mother,' she said, and added, 'We should get home. I came out to look for you, I don't like to leave Cal for long.'

'Your son!' said Anna. Then the questions poured out – did they need a healer, what had happened, had anyone harmed her, where was Brother John… They turned for home, leading the horses, and when they reached a stream Michael offered his hand to Anna, then to Thomasin, to help them jump it. His hand was warm, strong and familiar, and made

Thomasin feel she was where she belonged.

The walk home was long enough for them to exchange their stories. It was long enough, too, for a spark from the newly roused fire to fall on to the floor. The rushes smouldered.

'There's smoke rising,' said Michael suddenly. 'What's happening?'

'Someone burning rubbish?' said Thomasin. Nothing could be important now, not when she could walk home with Michael on one side and Anna on the other. She had to keep repeating it to herself – *It's Anna, she's alive, we are together, this is real, it is all real.*

The horses tossed their heads and twitched their ears as if they were uneasy. Michael was quickening the pace.

'I'm not happy about that smoke,' he said. 'Are they all out working?'

'Yes, of course,' said Thomasin.

'And Mother and Cal?'

'I don't know.'

Michael swung himself into the saddle and kicked the horse forwards. Anna and Thomasin took the other horse's bridle and ran, scrambled and clambered after him. By the time they reached the house he had wrung out his cloak in water to beat out the flames.

'I called,' he yelled, and turned to Anna and Thomasin with streaming eyes and smoke stains on his face. 'I shouted. Nobody's in there.'

'Jankin!' yelled Thomasin.

Anna covered her face to shut out the sight and smell and bitter taste of burning. She was fourteen again, fighting the unwinnable battle. Terror curled round her and into her like fumes, holding her like a witch at the stake until Thomasin rushed past her.

Thomasin! She shuddered, and ran after her. Together, choking, with stinging eyes, they dragged Jankin from the bed where he lay soothed and dulled by the smoke in his lungs, and laid him down on the grass.

'Jankin!' shouted Thomasin, and slapped him. 'Brother John! Wake up!'

'Get him to cough,' ordered Anna. 'Get his mouth open.'

Afterwards, Thomasin had time to think about how extraordinary it all was. As soon as she and Anna had come together again they had run through smoke to save Jankin, and she had known, as she choked and gasped, that she wanted him to live, he had to live, it mattered so much that he lived. Together, with watering eyes, they had bent over him, desperate to hear him breathe. When he did, they had hugged each other with triumph and wept together with joy.

By the time Cuthbert, Joan and their neighbours had arrived with firehooks and buckets, everything had been made safe. Anna had turned Jankin on to his front and was rubbing something on his back.

'Michael!' cried Cuthbert. 'What's happening?'

Joan came hurrying behind, balancing Cal on her hip.

'Is Brother John harmed? Michael, Tess, what… Are you safe? What's happened? Michael, introduce us to the holy sister! Sister, whoever you are, you're most welcome.'

'Mamam!' said Cal, and Thomasin held out her arms to him.

I have never seen anything more beautiful, thought Anna, than this flaxen-haired, smooth-skinned child with his soft little arms on Thomasin's neck and his cheek against hers. There was a sharp dart of pain at the way things might have been, but it was only for a moment. It was enough to watch

Cal. She didn't have to own him. He was kicking to be put down now, because he had caught sight of his father.

The door was left open to clear the smoke. Soot and dust lay in the air, staining the walls and the coarse sheets, dusting the floor with black, and griming Thomasin and Anna's clothes and faces. In no time at all, said Cuthbert, the bedding would have caught fire. Jankin tried to talk, but found it more painful than ever.

'Something about a woman and a child,' said Joan. 'And there's a cheese in the back, one of Chisholm's. The thing is, Sister,' she added quietly to Anna, 'he's not been in a good way at all. He took so bad after he got Tess and our Cal out of the water, there must have been something the matter before. Do you think that crooked shoulder could be damaging his lungs? I've often wondered if he was born like that.'

'No,' said Anna. 'I know a little about him. He had a terrible fall.'

'Well, it's a blessing that he survived it,' said Joan. 'Where would our Tess be without him?'

Jankin himself was astonished to be alive. He would have told them so, if he could. But he knew he was alive, not only because of the care of Joan, Thomasin and Anna, but because his work was not yet finished. There was still something to be accomplished and for this, his wrecked, pained body could go on.

He would have liked to look forward to a longer future. Anna was a skilled, gentle nurse. Even Joan envied and admired her. But not even Anna could take the nails from the cross.

Thomasin and Anna walked and walked, hand in hand,

that evening, along the fields, over the moors, and back to the house at Winnerburnhead. They talked about everything, but mostly, they talked about forgiveness.

'It's harder for you,' said Thomasin. 'It was worse for you.'

'It is now,' said Anna, and Thomasin looked up at her in surprise. 'When you're in a convent, and being cared for, and it's all behind you, and you think he's dead – and forgiveness is part of what you're learning, all the time – it's easier to forgive that way. It's harder to look somebody in the face and know it's him, and what he did. I'm not saying that I don't forgive him. I'm just saying that when he suddenly turned up it became harder, not easier. I had to start again.'

'I suppose we all have to do that, all the time,' said Thomasin.

The only smoke rising from the house now was the gentle wisp from the fire in the hearth. The night was growing cooler, and the house was warm and welcoming with a mixed smell of singeing, thyme, bay and goose fat. Cal was deeply asleep, his hair tousled, his thumb in his mouth.

'Brother John woke up a bit,' said Joan. 'He asked where you were.'

Anna and Thomasin stood over him. There was stubble on his face, and his breathing was hoarse.

'Poor sparrow,' said Anna.

Jankin grew stronger, finding peace and a sense of freedom as his breathing grew easier, and he could talk. Anna took over the work he had first come for, visiting the sick, and reported that there was nothing more serious than the usual summer sicknesses, made worse by the heat and dryness. She carried medicines and salves of mint, feverfew and chamomile, and her other simple remedies.

Presents appeared on the doorstep as if a friendly elf had come among them. There would be flowers and strawberries. Some called asking after Brother John, but Joan would not let them near him, knowing that he needed rest and quiet. When he was well enough to walk a little distance and had learned a little more about the Chisholm family, he knew what must be done. On a pleasant day, Thomasin, Anna and Jankin walked down to visit Mistress Alice Chisholm. They took honey on the comb and a spun fleece.

Alice looked sullen as she stood at the door facing the holy brother, the nun – and Tess Wishart. Alice's hair was brushed and tucked neatly under her cap and her clothes were spotless, but her eyes looked small and pink, her skin was pale, and a bruise was rising on her neck. Philippa clung to her hand.

'Peace be with you,' said Jankin, when he had caught his breath. 'May I speak with your husband?'

She went into the house without speaking and came back with Watt, who walked with the defiant swagger of a man ready to deny anything. Jankin drew him away, and the three young women were left watching each other awkwardly.

Say something, thought Thomasin, though she couldn't think of anything. *Say something*. She ought to ask if Alice was well, but she obviously wasn't. She didn't like to ask about the bruise, but she couldn't ignore it.

'Does that bruise hurt?' she asked nervously.

'What if it does?' demanded Alice.

Thomasin knelt to talk to Philippa, still huddled against her mother's skirt. 'Hello, Philippa,' she said. 'You do keep her beautiful, Alice.'

'She *is* beautiful,' said Alice.

'Yes, she is,' said Thomasin. 'I suppose it runs in your family.' Then, deciding she may as well get to the point, speaking very quickly, she said, 'Alice, if I've made life hard for you, I'm sorry.'

Alice still stared at her with resentment. 'You always got everything,' she said. 'You just turned up and got everything.'

'I didn't mean you any harm,' said Thomasin. 'And... I suppose if it hadn't worked out like this you wouldn't have Philippa and I wouldn't have Cal.' There was an embarrassed pause before she remembered the gifts Anna carried in a basket. 'We brought some wool – and honey. Oh, and the cheese is very good.'

At the word 'honey' Alice's eyes and Philippa's had lit up. Philippa loved honey. Alice fetched a small polished dish and put in a little spoonful, and while Thomasin dipped morsels of bread in it for Philippa, Alice sat down beside Anna.

'What happened to your hand?' she asked.

'I was in a fire,' she said. 'But I've learned to cope the way I am.' They both watched Philippa lick her sticky fingers. 'Philippa manages very well already. I hope you're proud of her.' They watched a little longer, and she couldn't help adding, wistfully, 'I always thought I'd like a little girl.'

Alice smiled.

Presently Jankin and Watt appeared. Watt was much quieter than before, and when Jankin said it was time to go Watt said his farewells kindly, almost humbly, promising to send some of his men with jars of their best beer to Winnerburnhead.

'I hope you'll come again,' he said.

'Yes,' said Alice. 'Do.'

'May we have your blessing, brother?' asked Watt, gruffly. So Jankin made the sign of the cross over each of them, and they turned towards the sun in the west, to walk back to Winnerburnhead. It was a slower walk than it had been on the way there. The journey back was uphill, and halfway there Anna and Thomasin pretended to be tired and in need of a rest, because they could see Jankin was in pain.

'We've made a start with Alice,' said Thomasin as they began the walk again. 'What did you say to Watt Chisholm?'

Jankin smiled down at his sandalled feet. 'That's between Watt, me and God,' he said. 'But I don't think he will ever hit his wife again. Keep an eye on her, Thomasin. If you're worried, just tell her husband to...' he stopped for a deep breath, 'tell him to remember our conversation.' He laughed, and stopped suddenly.

A spasm of pain crossed his face. They caught him as he fell. His lips still moved as they lowered him to the ground.

'Don't try to speak,' said Anna. 'Not if it hurts.'

'High... Crag... Linn.' The words were forced out, fast and tight, as if he knew he had to say them while he could speak at all.

'Take the next breath, Jankin,' urged Anna. 'I know it hurts to breathe. But just do the next one. The next.'

The next breath came so hard that she wanted to tell him to stop trying, if it hurt so much. But he did it.

'And the next,' she said.

His eyes flickered open. He smiled at her.

There was a long silence. She laid her hand against his neck for a pulse.

'Thomasin, run for Michael and Cuthbert. We need to get him home quickly.'

Chapter Twenty

Anna sat with Jankin's hand in both of hers, long after the pulse had stopped. She had stroked back his trailing hair, tidied the stained old habit as well as she could, and spread her own cloak over him. It had grown cool, and she slipped her feet in beside him.

All her life, he had been there. She had learned his name as early as she learned the words for rat, crow, snake, fox, fear, sword, blood, scream. As a little girl, she had prayed for his death until she felt that this was not something to pray for. Then she had hazarded everything on a marriage which was not a marriage – or was it? They had never been to bed. She had sometimes wondered if he was ever, in any sense, her husband.

It had been a strange journey that had led him to the foot of High Crag Linn and back, bringing the three of them together again, shattering their peace once more as he did it. And finally he had smiled, a sudden and astonishing smile that filled him with one second of beauty.

He had died without confession and without the sacrament, but all the confessing and forgiving had been done. It had all been completed before the sparrow finally fell to the ground. He looked rested.

'All's well now,' she said, and kissed him. 'Sleep.'

Thomasin arrived with Cuthbert and Michael, and two of the men. But when she came in sight of Anna and Jankin, Thomasin put out her hand to stop them.

'It's all over now,' she said. 'We shouldn't go near yet.' Not even she could go to Anna now.

'He wanted to go back to High Crag Linn,' said Anna. 'We should take him there.'

Brother John had been laid on a board on Michael and Thomasin's bed. Joan had insisted that he be properly laid out for burial, and had intended to do it herself, but Thomasin had seen the dismay on Anna's face.

'Sister Pentitentia will do it,' she had said.

'The nun! Tess! It's not decent!'

'She should do it,' said Thomasin, still watching Anna's face. 'They are... They were...' How could she speak the truth and hide it at the same time? 'Family. They're family.'

'Oh, in that case,' said Joan. 'Why did you never say?'

So Anna had taken water and herbs and a towel, and taken them into the room where Jankin lay. Joan fetched candles to stand at his head and feet.

With the straggled hair and lines of suffering, he looked to Anna much older than he had only five years ago. But, she realized, she had never known how old he was. She peeled off the rough old habit and saw for the first time the twisted and misplaced leg, the jutting hip and the crooked shoulder, pathetically white below the weathered neck. She could feel the broken bone beneath it. There were old grey scars from cuts, sword thrusts, and an arrow wound. She wrung out the cloth and washed him gently, finding that she was singing the Ave as she did.

'Hail Mary, full of grace, the Lord is with thee...'

The cloth grew grey from his face and neck.

'Blessed art thou among women and blessed is the fruit of thy womb, Jesus.'

She cleaned his hands, working the cloth between his fingers as if he were a sticky child.

'Holy Mary, Mother of God…'

He must have had a mother once. Washing him gently, she wondered what this woman had been like, and whether she had died young.

'… Pray for us sinners now and at the hour of our death.'

She found she was crying, and had to turn her head away. It wouldn't be right to cry on his winding sheet. It would have been easier to have had help with this, but she must do it all herself, using her damaged hand. She shook out the sheet and swathed him in white, with a pillow under his head. He could never had slept so sweetly in his life. Then she placed the rosary beads in his hands. That was all she could do.

They came in to see him and say a prayer beside him. Thomasin thought of Falcon, hacked to death and left to the carrion birds, and wept.

Cuthbert and one of the lads were to escort Anna as she took Jankin back to High Crag Linn. In a cool, early dawn, the men laid Jankin's body in a cart and covered him while Thomasin and Anna, saying little, prepared for the journey. There were ways of putting off the parting. One more loaf to wrap in a napkin. Oh, and we should send a gift for the hermit. But sooner or later Anna would have to turn her back on Winnerburnhead and walk away, and go on walking, further and further, until the door of the convent closed behind her.

'If your abbess won't have you back,' said Thomasin, 'you know you can always come back here.'

'She will,' said Anna. 'I'm sure she will, just this once. But I'll never be allowed to leave again.'

Thomasin hadn't wanted to hear that, but she knew it was true. She drew the back of her hand across her eyes.

'But you can come to me,' said Anna. 'We welcome visitors.'

'I can't leave here,' said Thomasin. 'They need me.'

'They could spare you, surely, just a few days!' urged Anna. 'You could bring Cal. He'd love it, he could play in the garden!' She imagined guiding Thomasin through the cloisters while Cal played under the fruit trees. 'I want to show you where I live.'

'Maybe,' said Thomasin, and already she found she was planning a trip, packing all she would need in a little cart, leaving the dairy prepared and the stillroom tidy, sitting Cal on a bundle. There might be another baby on her arm by then – but it was too soon to know. She found she was thinking aloud.

'When Falcon let me go,' she said, 'he told me never to come back. He called it after me – "Never come back!" But it's as if he knew I never could. You can't walk back into the past.'

She folded her lips tightly, and blinked. She wanted to ask, 'Why do I still want to cry when I talk about Falcon?', but she couldn't quite manage that, so she tried another way.

'Will you do something for me, Anna? It's about Falcon. He went against everything he knew, and all his loyalty, to set me free. I owe my life to him and I don't think I thanked him – and he died a terrible death, with nobody to comfort him. Will you and the hermit pray for him? Will you have a mass said for Falcon?'

'Of course I will,' said Anna, and added, 'I don't suppose you know what his real name was, do you?'

'No,' said Thomasin. 'Does it matter?'

Anna imagined asking a priest to say a mass for a hated

outlaw whose only name was the name of a bird of prey. Heaven knew who Falcon was. It was heaven's problem.

'No,' she said. 'It doesn't matter at all.'

After that, the point came when they had run out of things to say. The cart was ready. Anna and Thomasin hugged each other without words. Then, as surely as if a clock had chimed, they knew it was time to part.

'Just go,' said Thomasin.

Anna nodded and turned her back. Thomasin watched them out of sight, and stayed looking into the distance until they had disappeared. Then she smoothed her gown and marched back to her kitchen, finding the smell of the food unpleasant.

Brother Aelred saw them approaching, the two men and the nun, bumping and trundling the cart across the moors, and went to meet them. Before he lifted back the blanket over the dead face, he knew.

'My dear son, my brother,' he said, and his hand shook as he made the sign of the cross. 'The sparrow has flown. May God have mercy on him.'

Anna and the men stayed that night at the hermit's cave, and everyone's stories were told. Firelight flickered on the pale walls. The hermitage was, said Brother Aelred, consecrated ground, and a tomb had been cut into it for himself.

'There is room for Brother John too,' he said. 'This place will be more peaceful for his burial here. We will lay him to rest in the morning.'

'We're most grateful for it, Brother,' said Cuthbert. 'Then we'll escort this sister safely to her convent, and turn ourselves about for home.'

The noise of the rushing water kept Anna awake that night, and before anyone else woke she climbed to the top of the falls, struggling to manage the climb unaided with the skirts of her habit gathered as much as possible in her burned hand. She had promised Thomasin to offer prayers for Falcon. On the rough, cold ground at the edge of High Crag Linn she knelt, not looking over her shoulder in case a tall, tangle-haired man should appear behind her.

Thomasin didn't know how she came to be so wide awake so early, but it was as if the air sang. Something was about to happen. She dressed silently and walked out to the grey dawn and the early birdsong, facing the direction of High Crag Linn, gradually realizing what she must do. Near the stream, she knelt.

'Falcon!' she called. 'Falcon, I lived! Because of you I found love, more love than I could ever have expected. Anna escaped, and she's well. Jankin changed, and died a good death. We have broken bread together, and are at peace. So it's all right now, Falcon. I came here to tell you I forgive you for hurting me, and thank you for sparing me. I have a son. He's beautiful. And I might be carrying again. I'm going to tell them, I'm going to make sure they know what you did. Thank you, with all my heart, for setting me free. But I thought you might not be free, and I want you to be. I'll pray for you, though I'll always have to call you Falcon, because I never knew your real name.' She said the Lord's Prayer aloud, but felt she should say her farewell properly. 'So may God have mercy on you and, in the name of Jesus Christ, be free.'

It was as if she herself was liberated, as if everything around her was suddenly liberated, as if a cage had been flung open and a bird had flown free. Thomasin laughed out loud into the morning air and stretched out her arms.

At High Crag Linn, Brother Aelred woke, realized that Sister Penitentia was missing, and went to look for her. Finding her on her knees in prayer at the top of the falls he stood back, not wanting to disturb her.

The sun seemed suddenly strong, too strong for that hour of the morning. Brother Aelred gasped, widened his eyes and made the sign of the cross. Had there really been a tall man standing there? If so he had suddenly vanished, in a trick of the morning light or else in a blaze of glory.

Chapter Twenty-One

The girl visiting Hollylaw finally climbs the last step up to High Crag Linn. The weather has been dry, and she hears the waterfall as a steady gushing. Families are seated on the rocks with flasks, rugs and picnics. There is a safety rail around the edge of the cliff. Children play, chase and fight, parents take photographs, and finally they all pack up their rucksacks and cool bags and go home. The girl takes one more look, leaning over the rail to see the falls, and she, too, goes home. The shadows lengthen. The sun goes down. Only the waterfall remains, as it always did, and she knows that this is a place of peace and power, and that it was not always like this.

Hollylaw grew. The sisters of Hallowburn continued their work and prayer. Winnerburnhead thrived. Everywhere, stories were told of the terrible things that had happened when Hawk Jankin burned Hollylaw, and the Flower of Hollylaw died. Soon, every place had its own version of the story. Some had ghosts. Some said Hawk Jankin had been murdered by his henchman Falcon, and some said he still lived and stalked the moors at night. Some said it was Anna the Flower of Hollylaw who warned the village and was killed in the fire, and some said it was the maid, and others said the maid was murdered at the waterfall, and some said there wasn't a maidservant in the story at all. Everyone insisted that their own version was the only true one.

At the farm at Winnerburnhead, Cal grew up with his little sisters Anna and Joan and his little brother Cuthie. In the Winnerburn version of the story, told by Tess Wishart to her children, Falcon had been ordered to throw the maid down the Linn but had felt sorry for her and let her go, and she ran away over the moors and lived happily ever after.

Cal and the other children at Winnerburnhead learned a rhyme which they passed on to their children, and they passed it on to their children. It became well known in that area, and found its way back, in time, to Hollylaw. But after a few generations nobody really knew what it meant any more, though everybody thought they did.

Hawk Jankin at High Crag Tower,
Two maidens at Hollylaw;
The price of peace was a flower
That flowered nevermore.

And what became of the shadow
And what became of the bride?
And what became of Jankin
Who led the fiery ride?

Oh, one was lost in water,
And one in fire and pain,
And one went up to High Crag Linn
And never came back again.

All Lion books are available from your local bookshop, or can be ordered via our website or from Marston Book Services. For a free catalogue, showing the complete list of titles available, please contact:

Customer Services
Marston Book Services
PO Box 269
Abingdon
Oxon
OX14 4YN

Tel: 01235 465500
Fax: 01235 465555

Our website can be found at:
www.lionhudson.com